Stanley Salmons was born in Clapton, East London. He is internationally known for his work in the fields of biomedical engineering and muscle physiology, published in over two hundred papers and nine books. Although still actively contributing to the real world of research, he maintains a parallel existence as a fiction writer, in which he can draw from his broad scientific experience. He has written over forty short stories, which have appeared in anthologies and been serialised in magazines. This is his third novel.

www.stanleysalmons.com

Also by Stanley Salmons:

ALEXEI'S TREE AND OTHER STORIES
A BIT OF IRISH MIST
FOOTPRINTS IN THE ASH
NH_3

THE MAN IN TWO BODIES

Stanley Salmons

FINGERPRESS LTD
LONDON

The Man in Two Bodies

Copyright © Stanley Salmons, 2014
All rights reserved. Please respect the copyright of this work.

ISBN (pbk): 978-1-908824-40-0

Published by Fingerpress Ltd

Production Editor: Matt Stephens
Production Manager: Michelle Stephens
Copy Editor: Madeleine Horobin

This novel is a work of fiction. Any resemblance to actual persons, living or dead, events or localities, is entirely coincidental.

www.fingerpress.co.uk

In my writing, as in all my activities, I am blessed to have the love, support, and encouragement of my wife, Paula, and our children Graham, Daniel, and Debby. This book is dedicated to them.

THE MAN IN TWO BODIES

'What is a friend? A single soul dwelling in two bodies.'
   Diogenes Laertius, Aristotle

PROLOGUE

I'd never seen his mother before. If there'd been a funeral I suppose I might have seen her there, but of course there wasn't one. All the same, I spotted her right away. She was standing at the front of the chapel: tall, dressed in black, waiting quietly for the memorial service to start. She looked sad—well, I mean you'd expect that, but what I'm trying to say is she didn't look grieving sad, just terribly lonely. She held herself straight, like she was going to show everyone she was still in control. There were quite a few people around her but she still looked isolated. Even when she sat down in the front pew with someone on each side it was like she was alone. Nothing could get near enough to touch her.

You know how it is when you meet a mate's parents for the first time? You're curious to see whether they take after their mother or father. Well I am, anyway. It wouldn't have been polite to stare but whenever I could sneak a look I suppose I did take a more than usual interest. She was handsome, aristocratic-looking. The hollows under those high cheekbones followed right down and outlined her jaw. That and the wide mouth gave her face a squarish, determined look. All the resemblance was in the lower part of the face, I decided. He had a square jaw and a wide mouth as well. Also he had these two creases running right down from the cheekbones. Her mouth was set, and you could see she had two dimples in the same place. I couldn't see the colour of her eyes from where I was, but her hair was dark, almost black—unless it was dyed—whereas his was more of a straw colour. So I suppose the hair colour and the broad forehead came from his father. I'll never know that because her husband wasn't around. I don't know what happened to him. From what I understood she just had the one child and brought him up on her own. I was thinking how hard all this must be for her, but if it was she certainly wasn't letting anyone see it.

After the service was over, people filed out and a queue formed just outside the chapel, so they could say something to her before they left. I didn't know anyone there and I don't suppose he would have recognized the half of them either. I noticed there wasn't anyone representing the University, and I thought that was a bit bad, but I suppose they had to be careful about making it look like they accepted responsibility.

It had clouded over a bit by now and people were looking anxiously up at the sky, as if they might dissolve if a drop of water hit them. And then two minutes later they'd do it all over again. I suppose they just felt ill-at-ease, distracting themselves while they were waiting in the queue.

I wasn't thinking about the weather; I was wondering what I'd say to her. "Hallo, Mrs. Dukas. I'm Michael. I was a friend." That seemed too distant. "Hallo, Mrs. Dukas. I'm Michael. I was Rodger's friend." That was closer to the truth. Closer still if I told her we'd worked side by side. Only then she might ask me what the two of us had got up to in that lab. And if I answered truthfully they'd bang me up: in jail if they believed me, in an asylum if they didn't. So it's better all round if I keep my mouth shut. Which is a pity, because what we did together was truly amazing.

MICHAEL

1

Actually my Mum's the only one who ever calls me Michael; everyone else calls me Mike. And I never called him Rodger, either; it was always "Rodge".

We met in the first year of the course. University fitted Rodge like a glove. He was tall and self-confident and from day one he looked like he'd already been there for a full three years. The rest of us were milling around in those first few weeks, trying to find our feet. I certainly was.

To be honest, I wasn't sure I was supposed to be there at all. Physics may have been my strongest subject at school, but I wasn't brilliant at it, and the old place wasn't exactly top of the national league tables when it came to university entrance. So you could have knocked me down with a feather when Prince Albert University sent the acceptance letter, because physics is very big at Prince Albert. I was quite a celebrity with the teachers too, when they'd got over their astonishment.

Of course I started to wonder how I was going to cope. As it turned out, the first couple of weeks were fine, because they were covering stuff I'd already done at school and I was beginning to think, "Hey, this is all right". I didn't realize they were just bringing everyone up to speed. After that they switched to a higher gear and I don't mind telling you it was quite a struggle to keep up.

I made a few friends and we did some fairly serious

drinking in the bar down at the Students Union. Rodge never came; he couldn't be bothered with anything like that. He had a lofty manner and he didn't seem to need friends. The others sensed that, and steered clear of him.

I've no doubt there was a bit of resentment there as well. He could obviously cope so much better than the rest of us with the academic stuff. You know, he'd stick his hand up and ask a question in the middle of a lecture and I'd wonder how on earth he'd understood it enough to ask a question when I was still trying to grasp it at all. The lecturers soon found they couldn't fob him off with any old answer either, because he'd come back at them again and again till he was satisfied. He was hard on other students too, especially in tutorials. He had no time at all for people who thought they knew what they were talking about, but actually didn't. He'd argue them into a corner and make them look really silly. If it got too embarrassing, the tutor had to step in. Of course, that didn't exactly earn him a flock of admirers either.

After one lecture I was just as fogged as usual and I said to myself, "Hell, I've got nothing to lose". So on the way out I worked my way over to Rodge and moved at the side of him.

"You seemed to get the hang of that pretty quickly, Rodge," I said.

He didn't even glance round.

"It's not that difficult."

"Not for you maybe. But that last bit had me floored completely."

He stopped and stood looking at me, frowning. All the other students were pushing past us. I waited for the brush-off.

"That was the whole point of it. What was it you didn't understand?"

"Oh, I was all right until he got to Green's theorem. After that he lost me."

He looked thoughtful, as if he was working through the entire lecture in his head, which he probably was. Then he said:

"Well, do you want to go down to the common room and have a look at it?"

We sat down in the common room, and he took out a piece of paper and a fibrepoint and proceeded to work it through in a way I could actually follow. I asked him about something else a few days later, and again he didn't mind at all. It was really good; even the lecturers didn't have his knack of explaining things. By and by we sort of gravitated to each other. When it came to practicals we were expected to work in twos, and Rodge and I were an obvious pairing.

I tried to draw him into the social scene but he wasn't the slightest bit interested. So ours wasn't what you might call a friendship, at least not a normal one. We just expected to see each other every day, and we'd sit together in lectures and work together in practicals and go to the same tutorials. Come the weekend I never saw him.

*

There was an incident in the Final Year that's worth mentioning. We were covering a lot of nuclear physics at the time and Rodge had a difference of opinion with the lecturer. The argument went on a bit longer than usual and the others got restless, coughing and shuffling their feet. Afterwards Rodge and I took up our usual places in the common room and he behaved as if nothing had happened. Then Malcom Goodrich came by.

Malcom strikes you as being round in every way: round body, round face, round glasses. He's also on the short side, so as a specimen of manhood he doesn't have a whole lot going for him. Mentally—that's a different matter. As far as the rest of us were concerned he was one of the brightest guys in the year. So when he stopped by, looking at Rodge with a supercilious grin on his face, I prepared myself for fireworks.

"I must say you do come out with some surprising things, Dukas."

Rodge eyed him levelly. "I do my best." After an immaculately judged pause, he added, "Goodrich".

"You surely don't mean all that stuff about matter waves!"

"Every word of it."

He laughed. "The boys with the big particle accelerators had better pack up their bags and go home then. There's no future for that sort of physics. Rodger Dukas says so."

I glanced at Rodge. There was a muscle moving in that lantern jaw. A danger sign.

"I didn't say that. I said that particles weren't the only way of looking at matter."

Goodrich raised an eyebrow. Rodge sighed, then pointed at him. "Look, if you were working in optics—designing a telescope or a camera lens or something like that—would you be thinking of light as a wave?

"You know I would."

"And if you were designing solar panels? Would you treat light as a stream of particles—photons?"

"Yes…"

"Well, there you are. Light has the characteristics of both waves and particles. You simply choose the model best suited to what you're doing. The same's true for matter. For the sorts of experiment we do at the moment, it's easier to think in terms of particles. But it's only a concept. There'll be other experiments for which a wave treatment would be more appropriate."

"Schrödinger's equation?"

"Yes, and what flows from it."

"You're living in the Stone Age, Dukas."

And he marched off.

I glanced at Rodge, expecting him to shrug off the encounter, but he was muttering in a demented kind of way. I picked up the words "brainless" and "blinkered". I wasn't even sure he knew I was there any more, he was kind of talking to himself.

And suddenly his head came up and he looked right at me. His eyes are a sort of ginger colour, but very pale, so he always looks a little bit wild. But this was a really piercing look, and it made the back of my neck prickle.

"I'll show them," he said. "I'll show them all."

Even for Rodge it was a bit extreme. Evidently he had a bee in his bonnet about matter waves, but then he had strong feelings about a lot of things. I didn't attach too much importance to it at the time.

*

"That's it, then, Rodge. Last one finished. I can't believe it's all over."

We were strolling away from the examination room. We never discussed the exams themselves; it was a sort of an understanding between us. For Roger, exams were beneath his dignity anyway. I think he once called it "trotting out clichés so that the pigmies can match your knowledge against theirs". For me it was simpler: if I'd just made a pig's breakfast of what I thought was my best question there was no way I wanted to find out straight afterwards.

"You'll be off home, then," he said.

"Yes. I shifted most of my stuff last weekend. I just have a few things to bung in my suitcase. I'll go back tonight. What about you?"

"Oh, I think I'll go to France. There are a few people I can look up over there. Change of scene—you know."

"Well, I suppose I'll see you at the graduation, then." Something about his expression made me add, "You will be at the graduation, won't you, Rodge?"

"No. I shan't be coming back for that. You know how I feel about these pantomimes."

"What about your parents?"

"My mother you mean?"

"Er, well, yes—whatever."

"It's not for her to decide, is it?"

I was thinking, *it bloody well would be in our house.*

"I guess it's goodbye, then. Well, thanks for all your help, Rodge."

He actually winced.

"I didn't give you any help, Mike. We had some chats that's all. Anything you've achieved you've done on your own."

"Okay, okay, I found the chats helpful, is all I was trying to say. Right, then. Best of luck, Rodge."

"You too, Mike."

He strode off. No slapping of shoulders. We didn't even shake hands.

2

I got my degree: Second Class, Lower Division. Even though Rodge said he hadn't actually helped me I don't know if I'd have managed it without him. Don't get me wrong. I may not be lightning on the uptake but by the end of the course I could handle Maxwell's equations and vector algebra and Boltzmann statistics and stuff like that—even a bit of quantum mechanics—I couldn't have got a Lower Second from Prince Albert otherwise. But I couldn't push those things further, go beyond existing frontiers—I'm just not original enough. Whereas Rodge was, and you could see that right from the start.

If he'd come to the degree ceremony I suppose I'd have met his mother there. In a way it was a shame he didn't because everyone had their cameras out and it would have been nice to have had a picture of the two of us on the steps afterwards. Mind you, I was pretty busy prancing about in my gown, and my parents trying hard to look more pleased than surprised at what they'd brought into the world. I was the first one in the family to get a university degree so it was all a big novelty to Mum and Dad. To make things easier I booked them into a small hotel, and we had a meal and went to a West End show that evening. Made a bit of an occasion of it.

We're a pretty average family, I suppose. Mum and Dad have a two-bedroom house in Dagenham—that's right on the edge of London. Dad's a foreman in a local factory. They make kitchenware and he works on quality control. One thing we're not short of in our house is kitchenware, though I don't think there's a single item that doesn't have some sort of production fault. Mum doesn't mind. She says it doesn't matter what they look like as long as they do the job. She works part-time as a secretary in an accountant's office. She doesn't enjoy it much but she says it gets her out of the house, and the money's handy.

Dad is very stocky, strong in the chest and arms. He doesn't talk much, and I've never heard him raise his voice, but anyone would know at a glance it wasn't the best idea in the world to try to mess with him. He's put on a few pounds in recent years but otherwise he doesn't seem to change a lot. I suppose I take after him a bit in build, although I'm nothing like as strong.

Mum's very different: very energetic, always darting around, busy doing something. She runs the show really, paying the bills and making all the big decisions, like the move to where they're living now. Dad's happy to leave all that stuff to her. He sees his job as bringing home a regular wage. And substandard kitchen ware.

I have a sister, but she's much older than me. She married and went to live in Canada and we haven't seen her since. They've had a couple of kids out there. She stays in touch, sends photos of the family, and remembers birthdays, but that's about all. I was never close to her so it doesn't make much difference to me. I don't think Dad minds one way or the other, but it does seem to bother Mum.

"I don't know why they couldn't come over for a visit once in a while," she'll say, sighing over the latest batch of photos of gap-toothed kids with red-eye.

And Dad will grunt from behind the paper, "Leave them be, love. They've got their own lives to lead."

One way and another you could say I enjoyed my time at Prince Albert. I made a lot of friends and although it was hard I coped with the academic side, thanks to Rodge. But nothing lasts for ever, does it? Towards the end of the course I could see the time coming when I'd have to get a job and I thought I ought to do something about it. Actually I didn't need to exert myself too much because the companies who have a lot of vacancies for graduates send their people along to places like Prince Albert to give talks about how great they are to work for, and they'll often conduct interviews at the same time. The "Milk Round" they call it. I put my name down and that's how I got recruited by Telemax Engineering.

The pay wasn't marvellous at Telemax but they were supposed to have a good in-house training scheme. What that meant was, as soon as you started getting interested in what you were doing, and maybe even a little bit competent at it, they moved you to another Section. There were some bits I liked. The radiofrequency transmitter work was good; you got to design real power circuitry. But then they moved me to microelectronics, and I was spending all day in front of a computer, simulating what would happen if I ever got to make this little square of silicon for real. Then there was antenna design, which was quite interesting again, but they moved me off that into production engineering. And so it went on. You know those old war films where there is this planning room that has a big table with a map on it, and a lot of girls in tight blouses standing around it with what look like billiard cues, and they're pushing counters around on the map, moving a fleet to here and a squadron to there and a division to there? Well, that's what I felt like: one of those counters being pushed around. If anyone did have the big picture, they certainly weren't telling me. I stuck it out for two years and then I left. I worked in computer sales for a bit, but that didn't suit me much either, and I considered teaching, but it's not really my bag. On one of my visits home my parents asked me what I wanted to do and I just couldn't tell them because I hadn't a clue myself.

Then Mum had one of her bright ideas. "Why don't you speak to your Uncle Douglas?" she said.

Uncle Douglas is Mum's elder brother. He's the only one in the family who has a head for business. He ran this hospital supply company for a number of years and he landed a large National Health Service contract, so it did pretty well. In the end it was taken over and as part of the deal he left with a large lump sum. Now he gets his broker to make more money for him while he plays golf. I can't say the golf does much for his waistline, but that only adds to his general air of solidity. He's not so much large, Uncle Douglas, as weighty. If he sits down in an armchair it looks like it will take nothing short of a crane to shift him. When he makes a gesture it's only from the wrist. He reads the *Financial Times* and I think he's still on a couple of company boards, so he stays reasonably in touch with the business world. The whole family looks on him as some sort of guru; when he speaks, everyone listens, and no one dares to contradict him. You can imagine the sort of conversation I had with him.

First of all he told me it was time to make the acquaintance of the real world—you know, like I'd been living on Mars—and then he kept asking questions that could only be answered in one way—his way, of course.

"Where do you think the money is these days, Michael?" (I forgot to say that Uncle Douglas calls me Michael as well.

A lot.) He knew the answer to this one wasn't coming from my direction so he supplied it himself. "Venture capital, Michael. Mark my words. There are a lot of rich people out there, and they're looking out for ways of investing their money in new start-up companies with new inventions or new processes or new drugs."

"But I don't have anything new, Uncle."

A flash of irritation crossed his face.

"No, Michael, I know that. But there are people who have these things and they are looking for financial backing. And they know perfectly well that no one's going to give it to them unless they're covered legally. Inventions have to be patented, Intellectual Property Rights have to be protected, drugs and devices have to meet regulatory standards in every country where they are to be sold. There's your opportunity. It's an unlimited market for someone who has some scientific skills combined with expertise in those branches of the law. What you have now is half an education; what you need, my boy, is the other half."

Well, it seemed like good advice, and I didn't have any better ideas, so I thought I'd better see about getting the other half. I signed up for an M.Sc. course in Inventions and the Law. At Prince Albert University, of course—well, where else should I go? I knew they had a School of Business Management, and it turned out that one of the courses was tailor-made. I knew the ropes there, and I was a graduate, so getting admitted was no big deal. I expect you think I was just trying to recapture a part of my life that I'd actually enjoyed, and looking back on it I suppose you could be right, but at the time I thought I was making a career move. Don't laugh.

3

I suppose it won't come as a large surprise to you that I was soon sorry I registered for the M.Sc. course in Inventions and the Law. It wasn't that I couldn't cope; in many ways it was a lot easier than my undergraduate course. And I'm not saying it wasn't well run. There were bits of it that I enjoyed, like the training videos where a well-known comedy actor like John Cleese shows you all the ways you can screw up big time. But there was a lot of detailed stuff to remember, especially the case law. I've never been much for memory work. I mean, that sort of thing is fine if you're thrilled to bits with the number of nerve cells you've been born with, but I'm not, and it seemed pointless to take up the few I've got with all the ways businesses could get it socked to them for not covering themselves properly.

It was beginning to dawn on me that something was missing. Everything I was dealing with in the course was on paper: you either read it or you wrote it. I still hankered after doing actual science, at least getting my hands dirty with the more experimental side of it. I wasn't being unrealistic; I knew that academically I probably wasn't up to running my own show. But that didn't mean I couldn't work as part of a team. I could be a technician, something like that. I was pretty good with instrumentation. The pay wasn't all that good, and I dare say Uncle Douglas would have a fit, but at least I'd feel I was doing something worthwhile, something that actually interested me. The trouble was, I didn't dare to chuck in the course. I'd already had a few false starts, and it wouldn't look good on the old résumé if there was yet another thing I hadn't been able to stick at.

On that particular day there wasn't anything scheduled for the afternoon so I went for a stroll in Hyde Park. I walked for a long time and then I sat down on a bench by the Serpentine, and I thought about what I was going to do with my life. Some kids were around, sailing their toy boats on the lake. The wind was very changeable. A strong gust capsized one of the little dinghies, and it wasn't hard to spot the owner because he was jumping up and down and howling for his dad to do something about it. But then a nice steady breeze came along and drove two of the other boats along at a good lick, with the kids running excitedly alongside them. And maybe watching those little boats cruising along helped me make my mind up.

By now I was pretty nifty at knowing the least I could get away with, and I reckoned I could coast along without too much effort if I just attended the classes and handed in the assignments, even if they weren't brilliant. Once I'd got the M.Sc. I could either use it or do something totally different. Probably I'd end up doing something different, but at least I'd have the choice. So that's what I decided to do about the course; I was going to cruise it.

I wondered if any of the other students had problems like this, making up their minds about a career. Rodge for instance; I wondered what he was doing now. I'd lost touch with him completely. I hadn't seen him since Finals, and he'd never given me a contact address. I'd assumed he'd go on to do a Ph.D. but I didn't know where. The more I thought about it, the more I was curious to find out what had happened to him. Then I had an idea: I'd go and have a chat to Dr. Palmers.

Dr. Palmers was one of the lecturers on the physics course. He looked like he'd been a good athlete in his time, probably a distance runner. The really interesting thing about Dr. Palmers, though, was this uncanny knack he had of remembering all the students' names. There were over a hundred of us in first year but two weeks into the course if you asked him a question he would know who you were, and he would say something like, "Well, Mr. Barrett, what we have to think about here is…" It was great, really, not just that he could do it, but that he felt it was worth the time and effort. I've got to say, it isn't the easiest of times when you first go up to uni. I mean, you leave school, where you know the ropes and you know everyone and everyone knows you, and you're thrown into a whole new environment where you're not sure what's required of you, with a load of people you've never met before and who don't know you from Adam. You can feel a bit of a cipher in those first few weeks, and here was someone saying you actually mattered as an individual. I know it meant a lot to me, and the others probably felt the same way.

I suppose it was because he could be bothered to find out what our names were that he got lumbered with the job of keeping tabs on students after they left. So every time some daft Government Minister got it into his head that it would be nice to know how many students went into teaching, and how many into industry, and how many did higher degrees, and how many were sweeping the roads, the request would filter through the system and down to the departments, and he would be the one who had all that stuff at his fingertips for the physics students, and all the other staff could breathe a sigh of relief that this one had passed them by. So that's why I went and knocked at his door.

He remembered my name, of course. It took him about twenty milliseconds, but he remembered. He had stuff on his desk, so you could see he was busy, but you'd never think so, the way he got up and greeted me and sat me down. He wanted to know everything I'd done, and what I was doing now, and I tried to make it look like I'd deliberately acquired some industrial experience and had my career path all mapped out. Well it wasn't his problem and that's not why I'd gone to see him. He found my entry on his computer database and he sat there, typing in the new information, but I suspect it wasn't to help him remember: it was so he could respond to questions from daft Government Ministers. After a bit I took the opportunity to ask him about Rodge.

"Rodger Dukas? Yes, I remember him. Tall, fair hair, very intelligent. You two were friendly, weren't you?"

"Yes, but I've lost touch. I was wondering if you knew what had happened to him."

"Well, I've got an idea he did a Ph.D. here, but do you know, I'm not sure I've followed that one up? Let's have a look."

He started to tap at the keyboard again.

My goodness, I thought, *you are slipping. Only had about four hundred students come through since us, and lectures to give and papers to write and here you are telling me you haven't followed up Rodge's career.*

"Yes, here it is. Rodger Dukas. He registered for a Ph.D. in the engineering faculty: School of Electrical and Electronic Engineering. With Professor Ledsham. Now, has it been awarded yet….?" He hit a few more keys. "Yes, it was awarded last July. I don't know where he went after that, though. If you ask over at Elec Eng they might be able to tell you."

"I'll do that. Thanks very much, Dr. Palmers." I stood up to go.

"Perhaps you'd let me know if you find something out. I like to keep up-to-date if I can. Nice to see you again, Mr. Barrett."

I assured him I'd pass any information back to him. Actually I was wondering what the hell Rodge was doing in Elec Eng. I thought for sure he'd do a higher degree in physics.

I walked out through the big glass doors of the Physics building into one of those lovely spring days when the sun is just hot enough to warm your bones. It was too nice to hurry. Even so it only took me a few minutes to wander over to Elec Eng. There'd been a lot of construction work going on here when we were students. I remembered them knocking down the old red-brick Engineering Sciences block. Those Victorian buildings were so over-specified they didn't even need to sink new foundations—they just started again from ground level. Now I could see the finished result: a seven-storey slab of granite facings and tinted glass. The atrium covered the whole of the ground floor. I expect the architect was fishing for an award, because he'd designed it as a thoroughfare but it also doubled as social space; students were standing around nattering or sitting in groups on marble benches. There were islands in the floor with small trees and other plants, and low walls placed at right-angles to each other, and I suppose all this helped to baffle sound because it wasn't all that noisy considering the number of people around. The offices and labs were obviously in the floors above. I read the signs and found my way to the School Administration Office on the first floor.

The Administration Office was open plan: modern fittings, brightly lit—carpeted too, in burnt orange, with one of those hard-wearing floor coverings—so it was quite comfortably furnished, in an institutional sort of way. I don't know if the secretaries in the Office were really busier than Dr. Palmers but they certainly behaved like they were. I nailed one of them and stuck to my guns. This had to be the right place to come; it was where the post would be delivered. Someone like Rodge, who'd been there for three years, would be on a lot of mailing lists and he would still be getting post, and some of it might be important, so the secretaries had to have a forwarding address, didn't they?

Actually it turned out to be simpler than that: he was still in the building.

4

"I think I know the person you mean," the secretary was saying to me. "I can't phone him, though, because his lab isn't on the new network, and I can't take you there because I can't leave the office. Who did you say you were?"

"Mike...er, Michael Barrett. We were undergraduates here, over in Physics."

"Well if I give you some directions, do you think you could find your own way?"

I followed her directions. First I went out through a pair of doors and down a couple of floors into the basement. After the Administration Office it was like entering Eastern Europe. Well actually I've never been to Eastern Europe, but I've seen a few films and in my mind it was how somewhere like the old Stasi headquarters would have looked on the inside. The stone staircase led down to a dusty corridor with dingy yellow walls and a high ceiling all covered with ducts and cables painted over in the same colour, except it was about three shades darker because of all those years of accumulated dust and grime. The floor had been coated at some stage with a dark red material, all cracked now and gritty underfoot. Considering how warm it was outside I was surprised how cool it was down here. I was half expecting to see dungeons. All this would have been part of the original Victorian building.

I followed the corridor round and took a left turn as

instructed, and suddenly I was in front of a pair of wooden doors. There wasn't a lot of varnish left on them, and from the amount of scuffing I'd say they'd been opened pretty frequently with a boot. On the left-hand door there were a couple of empty screw-holes where there'd once been a label. All that was left now was a half-torn sticker; I could make out part of a lightning flash, so I guessed it had once been a warning sign for high voltage. I looked around me but this had to be the lab; there just wasn't anywhere else it could be. I knocked cautiously and went in.

It was a big room. What made it seem even larger was the way it was lit. The ceiling was very high and there was a bank of fluorescents suspended from it. They lit the middle of the room, but because the ceiling didn't reflect any light, the walls were pretty much in shadow. I could make out some cabling and switchgear and that was about it. The interesting bit was in the middle: there was a great cage there made of a fine copper mesh, and it formed a sort of room within a room. It was surrounded by equipment connected up with metal-clad cables. The air tasted musty, with a trace of that ozone smell that you often get around electrical equipment. There wasn't any sign of Rodge in the main lab and from where I was I couldn't see into the cage. If I got a bit closer, though, I could probably peek inside. I took a step forward, then thought better of it; if Rodge had just popped out for a moment and he came back and found me snooping around he wouldn't be best pleased. So I was beginning to think I'd give it a miss and come back another time when I heard a small noise. I said "Hallo?" in a loud voice and a door in the side of the cage opened and there he was.

"Hello, Rodge," I said.

"Oh, hello," he replied, like the last time he'd seen me

was yesterday instead of nearly four years ago.

"I was in the College, so I thought I'd look you up. I'm not interrupting anything important, am I?"

"No, you're all right. I can get on with it later."

There was a bit of an awkward moment. I thought maybe the best thing was to get him talking about his work. I waved at the equipment.

"This looks like a serious bit of kit. Those are lasers up there, aren't they? I've never seen any as big as that."

"Yes..." His mind still seemed to be somewhere else. Suddenly he looked at me and said, "Would you like a guided tour?"

"Well, yes, if you've got the time."

He led me over, talking on the way.

"The bits and pieces over here are test instruments, but the main bank there consists of oscillators and magnetrons and power amplifiers and they feed through to antennae inside the roof of the cage. It's all carefully matched, and they need quite a bit of tuning to get peak performance. These are high current sources for the photodiode arrays; you can just see the arrays if you look inside." He pointed. "See?"

We walked around to the other side for a better view.

"You're right about the long boxes: they're high-power lasers; they fire directly inwards. I prefer to keep all the major components outside the cage; they're more accessible for maintenance. Also these are continuous operation, not pulsed, and it's easier to keep them cool that way."

"Lasers like that cost a small fortune and you've got, what, eight of them!"

"Mmm. Actually they didn't cost me anything. You remember Dr. Ellis, over in Physics? Lectured us in Applied Optics?"

"Yes." I remembered him all right. That was another course I didn't understand.

"Well his group designs them. They formed a spin-off company, so all these are being produced commercially now. These were the prototypes. I just asked if there were any going spare and they let me have the lot. I think they were glad to free up some space. For them this is yesterday's technology, but for me they're ideal. They're not as pretty as the commercial item but they work perfectly well—actually better, from my point of view, because there are some adjustments you can make that were left out of the production version."

He opened the door of the cage and I followed him inside. There was a stout wooden table in the centre and when I looked up I could see that the antennae and arrays and lasers were all pointing downward roughly at the middle of the table. Rodge must have seen me take that in.

"Basically the idea is to generate electromagnetic radiation and focus it here." He put his finger in the middle of the table. "Of course, there's nothing new about that in itself. What's interesting about this apparatus is that I can do it at almost any wavelength from terahertz, radiofrequency and microwaves at the long end, getting shorter and shorter through infra-red, as far as the red end of the visible spectrum. All at high power. And I can operate all the generators at the same time."

Of course by this time I was itching to know what he was using all this stuff for, but it wouldn't do to rush it. I knew Rodge. Right now he was talking freely, but he could clam up just as quickly if he thought I was crowding him, so the best thing was just to keep the conversation going.

"God, that must take some power!"

Rodge looked pleased.

"More than a hundred and fifty kilowatts. You couldn't do it in a normal lab. Do you know what this lab used to be?"

"No, tell me."

"We're in what used to be the basement of the Engineering Sciences building. Forty or fifty years ago this was a metallurgy lab. They had several induction furnaces in here. The furnaces have long gone but the power supply's still here." He pointed to some of the thick cables I'd noticed earlier, travelling up the walls. "Those aren't solid cables; they're water-cooled copper tubes. They have to be; they carry a colossal current and the heating effect is immense. So you see, I've got power on tap here. And it's all three-phase, so the National Grid doesn't get unbalanced when I'm doing a run. It's not on for long anyway; only a few seconds at a time."

"And the screened cage is to prevent electromagnetic interference with other equipment in the building?"

"Yes. But not just in this building. When I'm doing a run I could make mobile phones squawk in Venezuela. I have to contain it."

"You know, Rodge, I've been wondering what you're doing over here in Elec Eng. I could have sworn you'd do a Ph.D. in physics."

"Well, there is an explanation. Look, would you like a coffee or do you have to get away or something?"

5

I followed him into one of the shadowy areas of the outer lab. It took a while for my eyes to adjust after the brightly lit cage but when they did I was surprised to see a sink and a kettle and a small fridge there. *Health and Safety haven't been inspecting here lately, then,* I thought. I mean, I've never worked in any lab where you were allowed to eat or drink in the same room. Just for interest I looked at the plugs to see if they carried stickers to say when the earth and fuse rating were last checked. Nothing. This place was amazing. In one way it was stacked with state-of-the-art instrumentation. In other ways it was trapped in a time warp. Rodge carried on talking as he filled the kettle and switched it on.

"You're right, of course, Mike: Physics was the obvious place for me to go. During Final Year I started to talk to some of the research groups over there about doing a higher degree. The Department is heavily into nuclear physics. As it turns out, an awful lot of that consists of designing and building special sensor arrays to carry out experiments at big accelerators like Grenoble. Then they get a few hours of beam time and spend the next few months analysing the collisions. It didn't appeal to me at all. If things went wrong with any of the equipment it might be months before you got another shot. I prefer to be in control of what's going on."

"You were keen on doing astrophysics at one time,

weren't you?"

"Yes, I was, because I wanted to study matter, and space is your alternative laboratory for that. But the situation there is even worse. You spend a year or more building an experiment, and then the launch vehicle explodes and it's all gone in an instant. Or you wait all year just for a bit of time on an orbiting instrument or a radio telescope. No, as I say, I like to run my own show. By the time we took Finals I still hadn't got anything lined up. Then I saw a Studentship advertised on the Postgraduate Noticeboard. It was in Electrical Engineering, with Professor Ledsham, to study the interaction of electromagnetic energy with living systems."

"The interaction of… that's a hot topic, isn't it? All these people worrying about what it does to you living under power lines or using mobile phones?"

"That's right. I think the big electricity generating companies are getting worried about potential law suits. So one of them funded this Studentship to look into it properly. I went and had a chat with Prof Ledsham. He was most apologetic. He'd applied for the grant months before, he said, and by the time it was awarded he'd been appointed Dean of the School. He didn't want to turn the grant down but at the same time he wanted to make it clear to me that he wouldn't be around much to supervise my work, that I'd be on my own a lot of the time. He seemed to think that might put me off. Actually that sold it to me more than anything else.

"There was quite a bit of bench money with the Studentship. I used most of it to buy good quality test equipment, like that high-speed sampling oscilloscope over there. I figured that way I could always build what I couldn't afford to buy."

"So did you build much of this, then?"

"Quite a bit. Not the lasers and more specialised stuff like that, of course, but a lot of the rest. It took about a year and a half to get it all together. But then I wasn't just equipping myself to do the Ph.D. work."

"What do you mean?"

"Well, I won't go into it now, but I had some other experiments in mind, far more interesting than Ledsham's study."

Again I wondered what it was that was so interesting, but he obviously wasn't ready to talk about it yet.

"Ledsham's project was just bread-and-butter stuff but I knew as long as I completed it I'd get my Ph.D. It wasn't hard once everything was up and running. To start with I used phantoms."

"Phantoms?"

"Yes, you know, they're sort of mannequins designed to imitate a human subject."

The kettle was boiling now and it clicked off, but if Rodge had heard it he was ignoring it.

"I measured field strengths and temperature rise and that sort of thing. Repeated it at different wavelengths and with different types of modulation. Then I did the same thing on real organs like brain, lungs, and liver."

I blinked. It was the casual way he dropped it into the conversation—as if playing with blood and guts was the most natural thing in the world.

"Where did you get stuff like that?"

"Oh, I got them from an abattoir. They were fresh enough, but still dead, of course. What I really needed was living tissue, with the blood flowing and all the normal chemistry going on. In other words I needed a live animal. We've got no facilities for that sort of thing here, and the premises aren't licensed by the Home Office. So I went over to Queens College and talked to the Head of Psychology there. He arranged for me to collaborate with a postgrad in his department, a chap called Tom Mayhew. There was a lot of paperwork to go through but finally we got authority to do some studies on rats. I couldn't move the equipment so he'd bring the animals over here first thing in the morning, and I'd irradiate them with the equivalent of having a mobile glued to your ear twenty-four hours a day, every day for a year. Then he'd take them back to Queens and do behavioural tests. I must say he was good with the statistical analysis."

That was rare praise from Rodge. The guy must have been a genius.

He broke off to make the coffee. He put a spoonful of instant into each mug, poured in some water, gave it a quick stir and added a splash of milk to his. Then he pushed the other mug and the milk carton my way. I picked up the wet spoon he'd used to stir the coffee and helped myself to sugar from an old jam jar with the label still on it. I tried to avoid the lumps. It wasn't silver service, but as a student I was well used to that.

"From time to time Ledsham would call me into his office to talk about progress. I think he only did it because postgraduate supervision is regulated and he had to set a good example. I could see his mind was always on something else. I'd feed him a bit each time I saw him, but what I gave him was only the tip of the iceberg; I already had more than enough results for my thesis. Doing it this way kept him sweet, though; he thought I was making steady progress and I could get on with doing my own thing. Tom Mayhew and I wrote a paper on the rat work and we put Ledsham's name on it. Really he didn't deserve to be an author because he didn't have the first clue about what was in the paper, but we thought it was the right thing to do, politically. And it gave him a paper to wave under the nose of the electricity company. But that's about the extent of his involvement. He hasn't been down here more than once the whole time I've been here."

He took a sip of his coffee and I did the same. It tasted like mud, actually, but he didn't seem to notice.

"After I got the Ph.D. I wanted to carry on with my own research, of course, but Ledsham wasn't so keen. Perhaps I was too independent."

I didn't know Ledsham but I could feel a certain sympathy for him. He'd be far too clobbered with administration to stay in touch with what was going on in his field or even in his own lab. If I was his research student I'd still give him a bit of respect. After all, the man's made it to Professor at a top university, so he's not a dope, is he? But Rodge wouldn't see it that way. He didn't make allowances: people were useful or they weren't. Not the easiest person to have in your lab.

"I managed to persuade him eventually, though. That was last summer. He's probably forgotten all about me by now."

All this time Rodge was looking at a point somewhere above my head and making sort of throwaway gestures with his hands like none of this actually mattered. He was always like that with people—it was one of the things that turned them off him—but usually he didn't act that way when I was around. I suppose it had been a while, after all, and he wasn't totally comfortable with me yet.

"Well you are pretty tucked away down here, aren't you?"

Suddenly I had eye contact.

"That's the beauty of it, Mike! Look at this place. Bad

lighting, old-fashioned wooden lab benches, peeling paint, bit of damp on the walls, no windows. There's no telephone or network connection because they didn't want the expense of running cabling down here. Nobody wants this place. Not when they can have light, airy rooms, white laminate benchtops and new lab furniture and over-bench power supplies and ethernet points, not to mention windows with a view. So they stay upstairs and I stay downstairs. It's ideal for me. I've got the space for the cage and the equipment, an incredible power supply to run it, and no one is saying 'Tut, tut, you're only a postdoc, you shouldn't have all this space for yourself and we need it for somebody else.'"

I nodded my understanding. I suppose I'd been so focused on what he was saying I'd forgotten how lousy the coffee was, because by now I'd drunk it down to a sort of brown sludge at the bottom of the mug. It looked like he'd finished his too. Still he made no effort to wind up the conversation. He seemed quite glad to have someone to talk to.

"What about you, Mike, what have you been up to?"

I gave him a run-down on what I'd been doing, more or less as I told you before, but I kept it short. Rodge doesn't usually take much interest in what other people are doing so I was flattered he'd asked at all, but I had no idea how long I could keep his attention. I hadn't lost him yet, though.

"I didn't really have you pegged as a sort of lawyer-cum-patent-agent. How are you finding the course?"

"Oh, it's all right. Well, no, it isn't all right, actually. If I'm honest, I'm bored witless with it. What I'd really like to do is research—not just development, real research—but I only got a Lower Second, so that's that."

He looked at me, chewing his lip thoughtfully.

"You could do a Ph.D. if you wanted to, Mike. There's a

shortage of candidates, you know. Once upon a time you'd have had to get an Upper Second or a First, but not now. And you've acquired some useful postgraduate experience."

"I know, and I'd probably enjoy it while I was doing it. The problem would come afterwards. I've got to be realistic, Rodge. I think I'm okay technically, but I don't see myself actually in charge of a project, running a research group. And with a Ph.D. I'd be over-qualified for the sort of job I can apply for now. It's different for you. When we were doing physics, most of were struggling just to pass the course, but not you. I always had the feeling that you were already looking ahead, equipping yourself to do something… well, something extraordinary, something beyond our horizon. I do envy you. It would be really good to be part of something like that."

While I was talking I was pushing a few grains of sugar around on the benchtop with my finger, lining them up this way and then that way, and not looking at him. Then he said something that brought my head up with a jerk.

"Well, I could certainly use some help here."

"Really? Are you serious? Team up together? Like the old days?"

"Well, yes, I suppose so. The trouble is I haven't got any money to pay you with."

We both fell silent, thinking about it. Then I said:

"What's your pattern of work here, Rodge? I mean, what time of day would you be doing the experiments?"

"Well, I like to work late, analysing results or doing calculations, here or at my flat—I always do that best at night. Then I sleep late, so I don't usually get in before lunchtime. I set up the equipment and do any tuning or calibration that's needed. After that I run experiments from about four o'clock to ten o'clock or so, depending on how it's going."

I considered it for a moment.

"Okay. Look, it makes sense for me to finish this damned course, now that I've started, and I've got a small grant to do it, which keeps me going. There's continuous assessment on the coursework and I have to pass a written exam at the end, but it's no big deal. The formal part of the course is over now; usually it's just a tutorial in the morning and then we get on with our assignments. If I do the bare minimum I can be finished by about four in the afternoon. Maybe even earlier. After that I could come over here and give you a hand."

"Fine, if that suits you. It would be off the record, of course, but I can't see anyone getting excited about it. Security won't stop you; there are so many students coming and going for one course or another that no one will even notice. And they never come down here, even when they're doing the rounds at night."

"Great. When can we start?"

"As soon as you like."

"Tomorrow?"

"Sure, why not? I'll bring you up to date on what I'm doing and then we can familiarize you with the equipment."

We got up and shook hands. I couldn't remember ever shaking hands with him before.

So that's how we got started again, the two of us, just like it used to be. Only better.

6

Of course I was very excited. I still hadn't the faintest idea what Rodge was up to, but it was Rodge, so you could bet it was mind-bendingly original. What if I couldn't understand it? I had to understand it! Rodge would soon lose patience if I couldn't follow what he was doing. I might have to read it up a bit. He'd told me what he'd done for his Ph.D.; that seemed fairly straightforward, but he said he was planning to use the same equipment for something more interesting. I could hardly wait to find out what it was. I just couldn't stop thinking about it and I don't mind saying I had some problems concentrating on my course. I sat through the tutorial with my mind elsewhere, and then afterwards I fiddled around with my assignment. Eventually I managed to complete it after a fashion and hurried over to Elec Eng at four o'clock.

Rodge was ready for me. It was clear at the outset he wasn't just going to use me as a pair of hands; he wanted me to understand what we were doing. He'd rigged up a sort of framework on a bench at the side of the lab. This was well out of the pool of light from the fluorescents so he'd brought over a couple of desk lamps. He switched them on as I came over and then I could see things properly. There were two upright retort stands and clamped horizontally between them was a piece of rope, which looked to me like a length of washing line. Dangling from the rope were two pendulums. They were identical in every way: the bobs were two-hundred-gram balance weights and the strings that suspended them were exactly the same length.

"Now, Mike," he started, "I'm going to take this step by step. To make it clear I'm going to show you some things that you've probably seen demonstrated at school but I want you to be patient, because it illustrates the very kernel of what I'm trying to do here. Okay?"

"Sure, okay."

He held one of the bobs and gave the other one a little tap to set it going.

"A simple pendulum," he said. "It oscillates at its own natural frequency."

He looked at me and I nodded. So far I wasn't finding this a massive intellectual challenge.

"Now, we can increase the amplitude of the oscillation by putting in a tiny bit of energy on each swing."

He tapped the bob very lightly at the end of the swing and kept doing it, so gradually the arc got bigger and bigger.

"But the timing has to be right. We can put in our tap on every other swing, that's to say at half the natural frequency, or at a quarter or an eighth and so on. But if we try to do it at, say, a third of the natural frequency we hit the bob in the wrong part of the swing, and instead of adding to its energy we dissipate it. What I'm introducing here is the idea of a resonant interaction, where a tiny amount of energy at the right frequency will interact with an object—the pendulum in this case—and make it vibrate or oscillate more and more."

"Like the opera singer who breaks a glass by hitting the right note," I put in helpfully.

"Exactly. Now let's add the other pendulum."

He lowered the other bob and steadied it with his fingers

so that it was hanging motionless in the neutral position, drew the other pendulum to one side and let it go.

I knew what would happen, because I'd done the coupled pendulum experiment at school years ago, but it is an amazing thing if you've never seen it before. The pendulum that starts off stationary starts to swing, all by itself. As it swings more and more the movement of the other pendulum gets smaller, until it's completely stationary. Then the whole thing repeats in reverse until the second pendulum is stationary again and the first one is swinging. It goes back and forth like that for ages.

We watched the pendulums doing this for a bit. I was trying to think what point he was making.

"Now, Mike," he said. "How is the energy passing from one pendulum to the other?"

"Well, obviously they're coupled by the rope. If you didn't have that rope connecting the two they'd be isolated and it wouldn't happen. So it's mechanical vibration passing along the rope that carries the energy from one to the other."

I was comfortable with this stuff. Like he said, it was physics we'd done at school.

"Good. All right, now let's go back to the single pendulum. Suppose, instead of this string, I put in an elastic band and pull the bob down instead of pushing it to one side. It vibrates up and down now, with a different natural frequency, but the principle is exactly the same."

"Okay."

"And if I replace the elastic band by a thick rubber rod, it still behaves in the same way, although obviously it vibrates more quickly and over a shorter range."

"Yes."

"Now I can't demonstrate this, but suppose we take that

rubber rod, and instead of hanging it on a frame we add a weight to the other end. So you have a rubber rod with a weight on each end. If we pull the weights apart and let them go, they vibrate in and out, a bit like before except that now it's happening at both ends."

He was using his hands to demonstrate the motion, his two fists as the weights, moving quickly towards and away from each other. He went on:

"What we're describing is a model of a simple molecule, consisting of two atoms—the weights—and a chemical bond between them—the rubber rod. Of course the vibrations are millions of times faster but if you want to set this molecule vibrating you still have to excite it at its resonant frequency. With the pendulum you could just tap it every few seconds. Here you have to inject energy at a much higher frequency, the frequency, in fact, of infra-red light."

I looked round at the apparatus on the cage, all the lasers and photodiodes, and back at Rodge. He was nodding.

"Yes, you're beginning to see the connection. Of course most substances are much more complicated than the simple molecule. They're three-dimensional lattices made of millions of atoms connected to each other by chemical bonds—like the rubber rods—and they can vibrate in different ways. But the principle is the same. When we feed in infra-red light at the resonant frequency we set certain atoms vibrating—like your opera singer with the glass. Each vibration has a different resonant frequency, so each needs a different wavelength of infra-red to excite it. In fact if a chemist wants to know something about the chemical bonds in a substance that's exactly how he does it: he shines a beam of infra-red light through it. He sweeps through different wavelengths, and each time he hits a resonant frequency the substance absorbs energy from the beam, so less gets through. That gives him a sort of signature for the substance."

"You're talking about infra-red spectroscopy, aren't you?"

"That's right. Now if you feed in enough energy you can excite a condition I call mass resonance. To explain that we'll have to talk in terms of matter waves."

I think a sort of shock went through me when he said "matter waves". I thought immediately of his argument with Malcom Goodrich and the way he'd been just after it. My nerves had started to tingle. He hadn't noticed my reaction though. He was warming to his subject.

"You see, at any one time, there is a certain probability that an atom will be in a given place. In mass resonance you spread that probability out so that there is a greater likelihood of it being somewhere else." He put his palms together and then drew them apart as he said it. Then his hands fluttered in one of those throwaway gestures. "In itself that's not particularly interesting."

"Oh. Why not?"

"Because in any practical situation the atom is not on its own; it's just one of a whole assemblage of atoms making up the material, whether it's a crystal or a piece of metal or a plastic beaker or whatever. All of the neighbouring atoms will be exerting their own pull on that molecule. So although you've increased the likelihood of it being somewhere else, in practice it can never take up residence there because it's always going to be attracted back into place by its neighbours. It's not an interesting situation."

"So what is?"

He leaned closer to me, and his eyes had a new intensity.

"What's interesting is if you excite them all at once, put all of them into mass resonance."

I thought about that for a moment.

"So that's why you've got all those lasers and photodiodes and stuff."

"Yes. And most of them cover frequency bands, not just one frequency, and I'm coupling and modulating and sweeping them. It gives you less power at any one frequency but I'm starting with a lot anyway, and you don't need huge amounts."

"Ok…ay," I said slowly, "so you get all the atoms resonating. What then?"

"Then you put in a nice big dollop of energy and it moves into a coupled mass resonance."

"Come again?"

"It's difficult to explain in words, because it drops out of the maths, but I'll try. I know, let's use another analogy. Let's think about a billiard table. Suppose you hit a billiard ball hard. It's running around, bouncing off the cushions all over the table. Sooner or later it's going to drop into a pocket. Once it's in there it's stable, it doesn't move. Now we can put in a dollop of energy: we bring our hand up under the pocket and whack the ball. It comes out of the net, onto the table and rolls into another pocket. It's stable again, but in a different place. Get the idea?"

"Not really. I don't understand where this mass resonance comes in."

"Ah. You see that's where the analogy is less helpful, because thinking about billiard balls makes you think in very solid terms. You think to yourself, 'Here is a ball, it can only exist in one place.' But theoretically it could exist anywhere. It's not actually confined to one place; it's just most likely to be found there. See the difference? And setting up the mass resonance spreads out the probability of finding it somewhere else."

"So what was all that about coupled resonance?"

"When you put in the dollop of energy the ball finds another pocket, but it doesn't actually move, it just spends more time in the new position. Think about the two coupled pendulums. Each one exists in its own place, but something is travelling backwards and forwards between them. Like you said, that something is mechanical vibration. It takes several seconds for the energy to pass from one pendulum to the other. In the case of the ball in mass resonance what is passing back and forth is a matter wave, and it's happening maybe a hundred thousand times a second. So you have the illusion of the ball being in two places at once. But it is an illusion; it's simply sharing its mass very rapidly between two stable states."

"You're saying that it's possible to transfer a ball from one place to another just by beaming a special kind of broadband electromagnetic energy at it and then giving it an extra jolt?"

"In essence, yes."

"But that's like a mass transporter—you know, 'Beam me up, Scottie' kind of thing!"

"No, it's not quite the same. I'm not saying that couldn't be done, but it's far more ambitious. As I understand it, the idea there is to take apart a person or an object to its elemental particles, send it somewhere and then reassemble it perfectly at the other end. That's heady stuff. All I'm talking about is each atom alternating its mass between two places. If every atom is doing it then the whole object is doing it. The constituent particles never lose their relationship to one another, not at any stage."

"But doesn't it take massive amounts of energy to do something like that?"

"Not as much as you might think. Remember we're not

moving anything really, just encouraging it to exist in two places. Look at the two pendulums. How much energy did that need? You just tap one of them lightly at the right repetition rate and it swings more and more. If the other one is there it couples to it and the energy flows backwards and forwards, for a long time. If you stop tapping it will all come to rest eventually because of air resistance and friction in the suspension. Those things don't affect matter waves. I'm not sure if anything does, actually. You need a fairly big dollop of energy to get the other state started, but after that it seems very stable."

I thought about all this for a moment. I'd been expecting something pretty mind-bending and I wasn't disappointed. I remembered reading somewhere in a magazine about quantum coupling. This sounded similar in principle. Maybe quantum coupling was the equivalent of what he was saying, put in terms of particles. I didn't like to ask; I knew how Rodge felt about particles.

Then I shook my head as if to clear it. *Come on,* I thought to myself, *let's get real!*

"I tell you what, Rodge," I said. "It's a fantastically original idea, and I'm sure it looks just great on paper. But I'm sorry, chap, it can't be done."

His face went very serious. He dropped his voice, speaking so quietly I could barely hear him:

"It can be done, Mike. I've done it."

7

My brain was in a whirl. I wasn't even sure I'd understood him completely. These ideas, these theories Rodge had been talking about, they belonged in the obscure world of the atom. Surely he couldn't have brought them into our world, the world we experience with our naked senses? I was pretty sure he could show me all the calculations, and I was equally sure I wouldn't understand them, so that wouldn't prove anything to me. I'm a practical sort of chap: I needed to be convinced by a demonstration. I think Rodge appreciated that, because without another word he took me over to the business part of the lab.

It was a pretty awesome set-up but as he went over it with me it quickly started to make sense. As I said before, the major feature was this big copper-mesh cage. It was rectangular. The shorter walls at each end carried most of the equipment: the power supplies, frequency generators, and amplifiers. From these a whole army of metal-clad cables crawled up over onto the roof of the cage, where they were connected to the various antennae and lasers. These larger items were mounted on a framework made of slotted racking, and all of them pointed downwards towards the table in the middle. Some of the cables passed through bulkhead connectors in the mesh to devices inside the roof of the cage. Other devices were above the roof but cut into the mesh. I looked again at the way he'd clamped the metal housings between flanges to make sure there were no gaps in the radiation shield. I'm a pretty fair hand technically, but I had to admire the job he'd done.

The control cables ran around the outside of the cage to the long wall, the one furthest from the entrance to the lab. Here they disappeared into a series of panels, with switches and dials and stuff like that. He'd identified most of these with little embossed plastic labels. I suppose if it had been NASA he'd have been sitting in a rotating armchair with all the controls arranged in a circular bank around him. His set-up wasn't as swish as that. He'd simply moved a long wooden bench up against the outside of the cage, and the various panels were mounted on that. You couldn't sit down to this one—you'd never be able to reach all the controls or read the dials. But there was an advantage in that. If you were standing up you could look over the panels into the cage, and if you got reasonably close to the mesh you could see what was going on inside.

The other long wall, the one you could see from the door to the lab, didn't have any equipment or cables on it at all—just the door you used to enter the cage.

He started taking me through the instrument panels and switch banks. Although it looked a bit complicated to start with, the controls were laid out in a pretty logical way.

"This left-hand half," he said, "is entirely concerned with the power supplies."

"The power supplies to all those microwave generators and lasers and photodiodes over there?"

"Yes. The lever switches here just knock each device, or group of devices, on or off. The knobs control the actual supply voltages, and there's a dial above each one to show what the setting is."

The knobs must have come from some pretty ancient equipment. They were big black plastic ones, really hand-sized. I like gear like that. It's got a real feel to it.

"All right," he said, "we've got a power supply to each device and we've adjusted its setting. That's all so far. At this stage none of the devices is actually doing anything."

"Yeah, I can see that. It's like switching on your stereo with the volume control right down."

"Exactly. What we need now is a way of controlling the output power that will actually radiate into the cage—the equivalent of your volume control. That's what this set of sliders is for."

What he was referring to looked like a sound recordist's deck in a studio. I could see why he'd done it that way. If you got all your fingers behind the sliders you could bring up the radiated power from all of the devices together.

"All right? Let's get this part set up."

We took up positions at the panel and he supervised me as I flipped the left-hand lever switches in turn and brought the volts up on each supply.

"Normally I'd do this at the beginning of an experimental session. We have to give it at least fifteen minutes to stabilize."

While things were settling down he took me over the right-hand half of the controls.

"Now this part," he said, "is concerned with what I referred to before as the 'dollop of energy'. As you can see, it's much simpler."

It was a lot simpler: just a row of lever switches with a red and a green indicator light above each one, and a large red push button. He explained it to me.

"It works on the same principle as a photographic flash gun. What we're doing here is charging a bank of capacitors.

The red light shows charging is in progress. When it's fully charged the green one comes on as well. The capacitors are under there."

He pointed under the wooden bench, and I bent over to take a look. I could see a row of metal boxes, about fifteen of them, each one the size of an old television set.

"Oil-filled capacitors," he explained. "Weigh a ton. Nice, eh? You know where they come from?"

I straightened up and shook my head.

"Remember I told you this was a metallurgy lab? Well, they held undergraduate practical classes in here, and some of them must have involved spot-welding. These were the power supplies for the spot-welders. They're really well put together—they have to be, they handle a lot of power. They were still here, all in perfect working condition, even after a few years of student use. I just took off the electrodes and linked them all up to my apparatus. They take about fifteen seconds to charge and then you discharge all of them at once into a separate set of generators. You deliver a huge whack of energy, but it's stored energy so you don't bring the National Grid to a stop."

"How do you discharge them?"

"Just one button—the red button. It triggers a circuit breaker."

"Not a solid state switch?"

A circuit breaker seemed to me a bit, well, last year. I didn't mean to sound condescending, but if I did it completely passed him by.

"No, a circuit breaker. It's over there."

He pointed to a box on the wall.

"Oh, okay."

Ask a silly question… the box was the size of a four-drawer filing cabinet.

"Right, that's about it for the equipment. All right so far?"

"I think so," I said.

"Good. Let's have a little demonstration, then."

He went over to the side of the lab and returned holding a glass beaker with some water in it.

"Open the cage. We'll put it in there."

He placed it carefully in the middle of the table and came out. I shut the cage door.

He disappeared over to the side of the lab again. When he came back he was carrying two pairs of plastic-framed safety spectacles. He handed one pair to me. The lenses had a bluish tinge. My eyebrows must have asked the question.

"You won't see anything, because none of it's in the visible spectrum. But there's still a lot of energy and the cage won't filter out all the infra-red that's bouncing around. It makes sense to protect your eyes."

I put them on. It was the only safety precaution I'd seen him take, so I wasn't in a mood to argue.

He didn't stand over me; he took a chair and sat off to one side. I appreciated that. It made me less nervous and gave me a better chance to learn the ropes. I saw him glance at his watch.

"I think that's enough time," he said. "Start charging the capacitor bank."

Mentally, I was still feeling my way. *Capacitor bank,* I thought. *That's on the right.* I reached out and flipped the first of the lever switches. The red light above it went on and I heard a faint high-pitched rising sound. It was probably an inverter, stepping up the voltage somewhere. I flipped the next switch; another rising sound. I worked quickly down the row of lever switches, and now there was a row of red lights and a curious little choir of rising voices.

"Right. Now start to bring up the radiated power. Slowly."

Um, the radiated power. That'll be the slider switches. I moved over to the left and used my fingers to push the sliders forward, taking it slowly. I glanced up because something had caught my eye. Just above the cage the big conductor cables came down from the ceiling and you could see them easily in the light from the fluorescent bank. There was a bit of condensation on the outside of the cables—I suppose that wasn't surprising with all the damp in here. But now the condensation was receding all along them and what had caught my eye was a line of steam coming off the cables. I moistened my lips. Okay, I was a bit nervous. So would you be. It wasn't so long ago they were using electric furnaces to melt metal in this lab. Those cables were carrying the same sort of current now.

The sliders were at the end of their travel. My skin was prickling. I knew it was silly but it seemed to me like the very air in the room was quivering with electricity. I tried to control my voice.

"Okay. We're on full power."

"Charging status?"

I glanced over to the right. The green lights had been going on. For each red light there was now a green light. *Full house,* I thought.

"All charged."

"Good. Turn off the charging circuits now. You don't want the capacitors recharging after you've pushed the button."

I flipped the row of lever switches back down. As each one clicked over its red light went out, but the green light stayed on. The capacitors were holding the charge. *Beautiful.*

"Are you ready?"

"Yes."

"Can you see the beaker inside the cage all right?"

"Yes."

"Okay. Get your finger on the red button, watch the beaker carefully and press the button."

I swallowed hard, found the button. Focused on the beaker with the water. I didn't want to blink at the wrong time. I pressed the button.

I heard a satisfying clonk from the four-drawer filing cabinet. That was all. I looked until my eyes ached. Nothing.

"Did you see it?"

"No."

"What, nothing at all?"

"No, nothing." I turned to him. "I'm sorry, Rodge. It didn't look to me as if anything happened."

He got up and glanced into the cage.

"Something's wrong. Bring the radiated power down."

I moved the sliders right back. I left the power supplies themselves switched on. I looked at Rodge, but he was talking thoughtfully, half to himself.

"Maybe one of the frequencies is off tune. It only takes one…"

There was a familiar fizzing, crackling sound—arcing! Both our heads snapped round and I saw the wisp of blue smoke coming from one of the boxes on the side of the cage.

Rodge started to say "Kill the supplies" but I was already flipping all the left-hand switches to the off position. We went over to the device. Rodge sniffed at the cooling vents and wrinkled his nose. Frying electronics have an acrid smell all of their own. I could smell it from where I was standing.

"Well I suppose that explains it," he said. "It must have been unstable during the run, and now it's decided to cook properly."

"The radiated power was right down, Rodge. Do they take that much power in standby?"

"Very little. No, it wasn't an overload." He gave a short laugh. "Don't worry—if one of the radiated power circuits had been involved you'd be picking yourself off the floor right now. No, I think it was a capacitor in the EHT circuit. They're not as well specified as they should be. It only takes a pinhole in the dielectric and they arc over. It's not the first time. I'll have to strip it down and replace the capacitor."

"Can I help?"

"No, not really. I have to wait anyway; there could still be several thousand volts on it—it takes a while to dissipate. I'll fix it tomorrow. It's probably just the capacitor," he said, thinking out loud, "but it may just have taken something else with it. Damn. That's quite an old supply so I may have to go on the scrounge for the components." He turned to me. "Look, maybe it's best if we leave it tomorrow, Mike. Let's see, what's today? Wednesday. Give me Thursday to get it fixed and come back Friday. It should be all right by then and we can carry on where we left off."

"Well, if you're sure you don't need any help."

"Yes, yes. Don't worry about it. This sort of thing happens."

As I was leaving he said to me quietly:

"You could say there's a plus side to this. You've proved your worth, Mike."

I was surprised and a bit embarrassed, especially as I hadn't a clue what he was talking about. I started to say, "What, because I cut the volts…?"

He interrupted me. "No, more important than that. You

didn't see what didn't happen."

I frowned and waited for him to elaborate.

"Some people's egos are so tied up with what they're doing they end up seeing only what they want to see. You, on the other hand, are totally objective. You always were. When we used to do those practicals as undergraduates you always had to be convinced of everything. That's good. That's going to be very useful."

I didn't say anything. I didn't need to. Our eyes met. We understood each other.

8

Okay, so things had gone wrong. It happens. Research wouldn't be research if things always worked. That made it more interesting, not less.

The incident reminded me of something that happened in a practical class during our first year as physics undergraduates. Everyone seemed to have got the result except us. I went over to the demonstrator, all crestfallen. He had a careful look at the figures in my lab notebook and then he straightened up. I thought he was going to tell me what a tool I was, or say "go and do it again". Instead he congratulated me on my golden opportunity. "Just because your observations don't agree with everyone else's it doesn't mean they're wrong," he said. "But what you're seeing is different from what they're seeing. So in what way is it different and why? If you can answer that you'll learn more from this one experiment than from a whole practical course that went without a hitch. We learn most when things don't go the way we expect them to." I know it cheered me up no end at the time, although it took a lot longer for the message to really sink in. I think he was only a postdoc himself. I hope he's a professor now; that was a bloody good thing to say to a first-year undergraduate.

Of course I thought a bit about Rodge's experiment afterwards but I can't say it bothered me. I mean, I didn't expect it to work in the first place so it wasn't that much of a surprise. I could see how it would annoy Rodge, though, because he'd set it all up for me and predicted what was going to happen. I knew from the debating incident that he didn't like to fail, least of all in front of an audience. Even an audience of one.

I went to my tutorial in the morning and after lunch I walked down to my bank. There are closer banks but all of us in First Year Physics, including Rodge and myself, had opened an account at this one on Cromwell Road. The reason was simple. This bank didn't have a branch on campus so it offered really competitive deals to attract the students. During Fresher's Week word got around they were offering interest-free loans for the duration of our three-year course. It turned out to be true. Everyone in my year signed up. The Manager was all right, too; very flexive. He's not there any more: maybe they thought he'd been too easy and moved him on or gave him the old boot. Anyway, I've moved several times since the course but I've kept my account at Cromwell Road so you could say their policy worked; it got them my business—for what that's worth.

I was going down there this afternoon to withdraw some more cash. To be honest that was only an excuse. There was a girl who worked there as a teller. Her name was Susan—I hadn't asked her; it was the name on the badge she wore. I don't know whether it was all that heavy chestnut hair, or the brown eyes that always seemed to be sparkling with amusement, or that low, teasy voice of hers, but she'd really got to me. I was dying to take her out, but how on earth could I manage it when the only place I ever saw her in was the bank? It wasn't like bumping into her at a club or a party or something. Girls are in social mode then: they expect to meet new people. But if you do the same thing when they're at work they consider it an unwelcome advance. And in a bank—well, she'd probably call the Security Guard and have me escorted out.

So I cooked up a little plan. My idea was to visit the bank regularly. If I made enough transactions we'd naturally enough start to pass the time of day, and it would lead to something more. That was the theory and that was why I was withdrawing small amounts of cash two or three times a week. Strictly speaking, I suppose I should have been using one of the ATMs on the outside wall, but if you don't want to do that the staff don't usually ask you why. So I'd turn up at the counter, and I'd give her my cheque book, and she'd ask me how I wanted the cash, and I'd tell her, and she'd give me back the cheque book and the money. That was all. It wasn't working. Our bank still had the old partitions and that made it even harder. How can you strike up a casual conversation with a sheet of glass between you? I realized I was going to have to make it happen, and that made me feel very uncomfortable. I'm a bit shy when it comes to girls, and of course that only made it harder. A girl like that, she could probably spot a chat-up line from a hundred paces. And she probably had a boyfriend already, although at least she wasn't wearing a ring. I know: I looked.

I decided it was now or never. I deliberately chose a slack time of day, just after the lunch-time rush, because I didn't want too many other customers around. I didn't know if she'd be on duty, so I scanned the counter quickly as soon as I walked through the door. I was in luck; there were two tellers on, and she was one of them. The trouble was, she was dealing with an elderly lady and the other teller didn't have anyone to attend to. It was going to look mighty strange if I started to form a queue when there was an empty counter right next to me. I went over to a shelf on one side of the bank and pretended to be filling in my cheque book. I waited there until another customer came through the door. Of course they went straight to the vacant position and I promptly joined the queue for Susan, standing behind the old lady. But at that very moment the old lady said "Thank you, dear", clicked her handbag shut and moved off and I found myself at the counter without even a moment to gather my thoughts. Susan looked up with a quick, professional smile.

"Hi," she said pleasantly.

I smiled back as winningly as I could and dropped my cheque book and banker's card into the scoop. She swivelled it her way. She tore the cheque out and scribbled something and I knew she was about to ask how I wanted to have the cash so I swallowed hard and took my chance. There was no one behind me, but I lowered my voice anyway.

"Could I have two tens and two fives and what time do you get off work because I'd like to take you for a coffee."

I had to get it all out in one; if I'd stopped I'd have seized up totally. Then I held my breath, prepared to become the most miserable young man in South Kensington, possibly the world.

She stopped dead for an instant, and lowered and raised thick eyelashes.

"Two tens and two fives," she repeated. "And I believe there was something else, which I didn't quite catch."

I tried to sound engaging. Actually I can do engaging.

"Please don't make me say it again. It took all my courage to get it out the first time."

She glanced to her right to see if the conversation was being overheard, but the other teller was still dealing with her customer. She looked straight up at me. Her eyes were very dark and solemn, but her voice still had that teasy quality that made things go buzz-buzz inside me.

"You're serious, aren't you?"

"Yes, I'm deadly serious. I want to take you for a coffee."

"Just a coffee?"

Apart from giving herself thinking time, I knew what she meant. I chose to ignore the innuendo.

"Well," I said brightly, "I could run to a Danish if you fancy something with it."

She tried to suppress the smile but she couldn't manage it entirely. *God*, I thought, *she has dimples too!* She glanced again at my cheque book to register the name. Then she dropped it, and the cash, into the scoop, and sat up primly, her slim hands on the desk in front of her.

"All right, Mr. Barrett," she said suddenly, "quarter past five."

Like she was making a business appointment.

I couldn't believe it. I only just stopped myself from thanking her.

"I'll wait for you outside," I said quietly, and hurried out before I made a worse fool of myself.

There was a nice cool breeze coming down the street. It made me realize how hot my face was.

9

I made sure I was there before time. It wasn't difficult; I'd been looking at my watch all afternoon. She came through the door on the dot of quarter past five, wearing a navy suit, with a black handbag over one shoulder. She hadn't been wearing a jacket in the bank. Now that she was out from behind the counter I could see she was quite petite. That was a relief. I'm not all that tall myself and I wouldn't have wanted her towering over me. And she wore a skirt, knee-length. That was good too: I feel intimidated by women who wear business suits with trousers. It may sound silly, but it's that whole "female executive" thing. If I'm looking for a boy-girl relationship I don't want them to treat me as a management problem.

I stepped up right away.

"Hi," I said awkwardly.

"Hallo." Her manner was friendly, but a bit guarded.

"Er, do you have any preference about where to go, or shall I choose?"

"Well, to be frank, Mr. Barrett…"

"Oh, Mike, please. Everyone calls me Mike… Susan. Is it okay if I call you Susan?"

"Suzy. Only my Mum calls me Susan."

"Oh, right. My Mum calls me Michael."

We laughed, and then sort of caught ourselves.

"Mike," she said. "What I wanted to say is, we've got a

coffee machine in the bank so it's on tap all day long. If I have any more I'll overdose on caffeine."

"Oh."

I must have looked as crestfallen as I felt.

"There's a nice wine bar near South Ken' station. Shall we go there?"

"Great idea," I said. "I don't know why I didn't think of that. Well, I do know. I wouldn't have wanted to suggest it to you."

"Well, don't get the wrong idea. I just thought it would be nice to have a little aperitif instead."

I was thinking, *I can't seem to say the right thing. It's like walking through a bloody minefield.*

"I'll pay my way," she added.

"Oh, no, er—my invitation, my shout."

It was a relief to set off in the direction of South Kensington. I was thinking of her "Just a coffee?" remark. She should be feeling more relaxed about that now; if I was trying to abduct her I'd be opening the door of an Aston Martin or something. The pavement was crowded, and it was pretty much impossible to walk side by side; mostly I let her lead and I followed. What with this and people pushing past and lorries and buses thundering by and I didn't even try to keep up a conversation.

Ten minutes later we were at the wine bar. As soon as we got inside the second entrance door the noise of the traffic was suddenly snuffed out. The lighting was low and there was some quiet jazz playing. A group of customers in one corner had quite loud voices so we chose a table well away from them. I sat down opposite her and tried to smile. My chest was fluttering like there was a bird trapped inside it. I'd had the same feeling a couple of times before, when I was waiting for my turn in a viva exam or an interview. It was downright unpleasant then. This was, too, but in an enjoyable sort of way. I knew I ought to be saying something but my mouth seemed to have dried up. Thank goodness the waiter came over quickly and I had a chance to gather my scattered wits. Suzy ordered a New Zealand Sauvignon Blanc. I just said I'd have the same and he went off. I was sweating a bit from the walk, so I said:

"Do you mind if I take my jacket off?"

"No, go ahead. I'll do the same."

I got up and hung my jacket over the back of the chair. She took her jacket off and turned in her chair to hang it over the back. As she did so her breast tightened and the shadow of a white lacy undergarment showed briefly under the fabric of her blouse. I averted my eyes with difficulty. Everything about her was so utterly desirable. She turned back to the table and waited for me to open the conversation.

I still couldn't think of anything to say. Half of me could hardly believe I'd got this far; the other half was wondering how long it would be before I put my size nine right in it and spoiled everything. The first thing that leapt into my head was, "Do you come here often?" I just managed to stop myself. *Great opener, Mike. You're asking her if she spends all her time in wine bars.* How about, "I don't usually pick up strange women"? *Oh, brilliant, Mike. That makes her both strange and a pick-up.* "I don't do this every day"? *Wonderful. Only every other day. Try again. Perhaps introduce yourself properly...*

"I opened an account at your bank when I was a student here. I've come back to do a postgraduate course."

"What in?" She sounded curious.

"It's an M.Sc. in Inventions and the Law."

"Sounds interesting."

"Well, to be honest it sounds more interesting than it actually is."

"What did you do for your first degree, then?"

"Physics."

"Oh. I was never much good at physics. I did geography."

"You did a degree in geography?"

From the way she stiffened I knew I'd sounded too surprised. Maybe she thought I was saying "A chap doesn't expect a mere bank teller to have a degree." I didn't mean to—I was just tip-toeing through the minefield again. I covered myself quickly.

"It's just that I would have expected something more like accountancy or an MBA."

She relaxed a bit, and I breathed again.

"No, I wasn't planning to go for a career in banking. I started doing a PGCE… "

"That's a Postgraduate Certificate of Education? You wanted to be a teacher?"

"Yes. But when I started my placement I soon realized I'd made a mistake. The kids played me up dreadfully. They didn't want to learn. I took this job because it paid, and there was a training element. And I did economic geography, so it wasn't completely irrelevant."

I nodded. I could have listened to her for ever but I realised it was my turn.

"I did a stint in industry, but I couldn't get on with that either. Every time I got interested in something they moved me on. I enrolled on this course but now I'm not sure that's for me, either. I can cope with it; it just doesn't grab me, somehow."

The waiter brought the glasses and poured the wine. It

was nicely chilled. She lifted it to her nose and I did the same. It smelt of pineapple and gooseberries. I took a sip. It had a lovely refreshing zing to it, like that stuff that sprays off when you peel a lemon. I tried to relax a little.

"Being a geographer, you'll know precisely in the world where this comes from, I suppose." I grinned at her.

She accepted the challenge without hesitation.

"Marlborough. North-east corner of the South Island of New Zealand."

"Ever been there?"

"No. I haven't been to Australia or New Zealand. I've been to South America, though. Costa Rica."

"Wow, that's pretty exotic. How did that come about?"

"Well, in my third year I did a project on management of natural resources in Central American economies. I used Costa Rica as an example. I got really interested. So after my exams I went on a youth adventure course. I spent three months there. My parents paid for it. A sort of graduation present, although they gave it to me before the results were out, bless them. It was wonderful."

Her dark eyes were dreamy. The pupils were just huge. We sipped some more wine. I tried not to take too much. I figured the longer it lasted the longer I could keep her there. She might not be up for a second glass.

"I'd like to do a bit more travelling," I said. I've only ever got as far as the continent. I did one of those Eurorail trips during my second long vacation. Covered quite a bit of ground. It was good fun."

I could see that the conversation was running out. I didn't want any more awkward silences so I ran on a bit.

"I'm helping out with a bit of research in my spare time. A friend of mine is a postdoc here, so I'm lending a hand."

"What are you doing?"

She would ask that, of course. I'd been stupid to go there.

"Well, it's a bit complicated. It has to do with the physics of matter."

"Oh. You must be very bright."

"Who, me? No, not me! Rodge is the brains behind it. I'm just a hack technician. It's good, though. It's what I'd really like to be involved in if I had half a chance. You know, something where each day is different, each day brings something unexpected. Even if it's a problem."

I was thinking about the burnt out capacitor. She was nodding and it dawned on me, uncomfortably, that her job must be pretty routine. So I asked:

"Do you, er, like what you're doing? Your job?"

"It's all right. I've been with them for nearly four years now so the novelty's wearing thin. But there's scope for advancement."

"You seem to enjoy it. I mean, you're good with customers. When you look after me I always go out feeling ten feet tall."

She laughed, and I felt ridiculously pleased.

"A job's as interesting as you make it. But it can drive you up the wall a bit at times. We had a busy lunch hour, with queues on every position, and I had to deal with someone paying in. Counting coins and putting them into bags with everyone tutting and tapping their feet."

"And then an impertinent young man asks you out for coffee."

She pursed her lips in a rueful smile. "I could hardly believe your nerve. But it did brighten up my afternoon. Thanks for that."

It looked like we might be heading for an awkward silence again, so I asked her to tell me a bit more about Costa Rica.

As I expected, she didn't need a whole lot of encouragement. I asked her about the climate, the plant life, whether there were problems with deforestation, like in Brazil. I knew I was on my back foot here, not knowing anything about South America, but I wasn't too bothered. Everyone has holes in their knowledge; it shouldn't stop you asking reasonably intelligent questions as long as you're actually interested in the answers, and I was. There's a difference between being ignorant and being stupid. I asked her about the insects; I'd heard they have some huge ones there. She said she hadn't come across any, except for the big butterflies. That was a relief; I can cope with butterflies.

She finished her wine, flicked a paper napkin out of a little stack on the table, dabbed it around her mouth and put it on the table. Just seeing the traces of lipstick on it made my heart bang. She glanced at a dainty wristwatch. I knew what was coming.

"Look, this has been lovely but I've got to be on my way."

"Sure, whatever. Have you got far to go?"

"No, not far. Notting Hill. I share a flat with a girlfriend. What about you?"

"I rent a flat in Queens Gate. It's very handy for the college. Er, look Suzy, I'd love to see you again, but I don't want to push my company if you're already seeing someone."

"I'm a free agent."

Internally I breathed a sigh of relief.

"So could we do something like this again?"

"Okay. But I pay my way. Understood?"

"Yeah, sure. Great. Oh, by the way, it's a little embarrassing to ask you at the bank. Is there some other way I can contact you?"

She laughed and I guessed she was remembering how

awkward I must have looked on the other side of the glass.

"I'll give you my mobile number," she said, and wrote it on the paper napkin that was lying on the table. Then she noticed the lipstick marks and realized it was the one she'd already used.

"Oh, sorry…" She reached for another one.

"No, that's fine," I said firmly, picking up the napkin.

"I'll walk you down to the station," I said, reaching for my jacket and making sure that the paper napkin was tucked securely into the pocket.

10

On Friday afternoon I walked briskly over to Electrical Engineering. It was another clear, warm day, and my eyes hurt from the sunlight reflecting off the glazed façades. After that, going down the stairs to Rodge's lab was like descending into the underworld.

I asked him about the power supply that had cooked but he dismissed it quickly; he'd only had to replace the capacitor and it was working fine now. In fact he already had the power supplies running at voltage. He was impatient to do the experiment again.

We went into the cage. He'd put two empty glass beakers in there, and they were sitting in the middle of the table. He took a water bottle and filled each one about two-thirds full. Then he picked up a brown glass chemical bottle; I couldn't see the label. He unscrewed the cap and gently shook a few small purple crystals into the palm of his hand. I recognized them straight away: potassium permanganate.

"A small refinement," he said.

He tipped the purple permanganate crystals into the water in one beaker. A little plume of colour curled up from the crystals, like smoke from a chimney. He swirled the beaker slightly and put it down. He picked up the other beaker; obviously he wasn't planning to leave that one in the cage.

"This can be for comparison," he said. "You'll see why later. Ready?"

I was, of course, so I put on the protective specs and took up my position at the panel and went through the same sequence as before, charging the capacitors until the green lights came on, putting all my fingers behind the sliders to bring up the radiated power, then switching off the charging circuits so that the red lights went out. Rodge wasn't sitting down this time; he was watching my moves, but he still wasn't hanging over me. He hadn't said anything, so I put my finger on the red button and glanced back at him.

"Okay to go ahead?"

"Yes. Watch carefully."

Well, I'd heard that one before but all the same I watched carefully and pushed the button, and the four-drawer filing cabinet went clonk, and then something seemed to go wrong with my eyes.

A moment ago there had been one beaker of water; now there were two, about two feet apart. Each of them had an identical little curl of purple smoke from the permanganate crystals. I tried to rub my eyes, forgetting I was wearing the protective spectacles, and knocked them onto the floor. I picked them up, but just before I put them on again I sneaked a quick look into the cage. No, it was nothing to do with the specs; there were still two beakers there.

I looked round a little desperately at Rodge. He was standing there, the comparison beaker still on the bench next to him. He didn't need to ask what I'd seen; my expression must have said it all.

"All right," he said, "you can bring the radiated power down now."

I pulled the sliders swiftly back to the zero position, expecting the two images to become one. They were still there. I felt a moment of panic. Again I turned to Rodge.

"Interesting, isn't it?" he said, with a tolerant smile. "But if you think about it, it's to be expected. Like I said, there's no friction or other influence to wind down the energy in the matter waves so the resonance is quite stable. I've had it going for hours."

"Then for God's sake how do you stop it?"

"Do you see a power supply there labelled 'OH'?"

For each power supply there was a dial with a black plastic knob underneath it, and between the two was a small embossed label. I scanned the labels and found one that said "–OH".

"Okay, got it."

"Right. Now follow this sequence. Three steps. One, bring the radiated power up again. Two, reduce the voltage on that supply by fifty volts. Three, bring the power smoothly down again."

I advanced the sliders, then turned the large knob under the "–OH" label anti-clockwise, bringing the needle on the dial down, and then pulled smoothly back on the sliders. I checked on the cage and did a double take. There was only one beaker.

I turned to him again, questions all over my face.

"I'll explain. You remember what I told you before? Every substance is held together by chemical bonds. We're using broad spectrum electromagnetic radiation to put all of those bonds into resonance, right?"

I nodded.

"Well," he continued, "the radiation sources are in groups, each group connected to a different power supply. I've given each supply a name—for convenience it's the name of the most important chemical bond in that group."

He tapped the large black knob labelled "-OH".

"This supply includes the –OH bond. Water is absolutely chock full of them. When you take it off its proper working voltage you detune the radiation enough to take that bond off resonance. So the mass resonance collapses on that one and it drags all the others back with it. Simple as that."

"I see," I said weakly.

"Now, there's something else I want to show you. Come into the cage."

On the way in he picked up the second beaker and an instrument with a probe dangling on a lead. It turned out to be an electronic thermometer. He dropped the probe into the beaker on the table in the cage and we read the display. Of course it was easy enough to keep track of which beaker was which, because he'd only put the permanganate crystals into the one in the cage. The thermometer registered 24.3°C. Then he dropped the probe into the second beaker, the one he'd kept outside the cage. The temperature in that one was 24.2°C. The difference in temperature was only 0.1°C.

"You see? All that energy focused on it and it barely rises in temperature. That's because the conditions are optimized for harnessing the energy as matter waves instead of heat."

"That's impressive," I said.

I meant it. Actually I was blown away by what I'd seen. And there were loads of questions clambering into my mind.

"Rodge, that power supply I turned down. You said it affected the –OH bond. But glass doesn't have any of those bonds, does it? I thought it was basically silicon dioxide. Why doesn't the water shift and leave the beaker behind?"

"It doesn't matter which bond you detune. As soon as a resonance collapses it drags everything back with it. Where the water goes the beaker has to follow. If you detuned the bonds in the glass, the beaker would go and the water would follow. The atoms have to keep their relationship with each other."

I nodded slowly. I was beginning to get the hang of this. But there were still things that bothered me.

"Those beakers, when they were, er, in mass resonance. They were a couple of feet apart. Why that distance? Why not an inch? Why not a mile?"

"Good question. It seems to depend on the size of the dollop of energy you inject when you set up the resonant state, but I haven't been able to work out what the precise relationship is. That's one of the things you could help me with. Of course we're only working with a fraction of the available power. I'm talking about the right-hand bank now—you know, the part that charges the capacitors."

"Yeah, I knew what you meant. What about direction? Why does the second beaker appear along the bench. Why not in another direction, like towards the door?"

"Another good question. The dollop of energy we put in, it's in the form of electromagnetic waves, like the rest, but they're plane polarized. At the moment I've got the plane parallel to the length of the cage. I could change it if I wanted to, and then they'd separate in a different direction."

"Okay. And so far as you know those two beakers would have gone on like that, existing side by side, forever?"

"Well I've only tested it for a few hours, but I don't see why it shouldn't go on for days and weeks. I don't know of anything that absorbs matter waves."

"That's something else we ought to look at."

"You're right, Mike, we should. It would be easy enough. All we need to do is drop various materials in the beam and see what happens. Actually there's a cupboard here full of materials samples. Shall we take a look?"

He turned and went out of the cage. Just before following him I passed a hand quickly over the table, where that mysterious second beaker had appeared. I didn't think Rodge was the sort to go in for conjuring tricks but I needed to reassure myself. There was nothing there. I followed him over to the other side of the lab, where the pendulums were set up. He was opening a cupboard under the bench. It was the wrong one so he closed it and opened another. He reached inside and came out with some rectangular sheets, which he put on the bench near the desk lamps so that we could see them. They were all the same size, about as big as a glossy magazine but only a millimetre or two thick. Some were metal, some looked like plastic.

"Metallurgy again. I think these were test materials for practical classes. They probably used them to compare metals with other common materials."

I had a closer look. Each one had the details of the material written on them in spirit marker. Taking four from the top of the pile I saw "Nickel 100%", "Methyl methacrylate", "PTFE", "Martensitic steel 15% chromium, 1% carbon", "Methyl methacrylate"—ah, so there were repeats. You'd expect that from practical class materials. I thought about it for a moment and then turned to Rodge.

"I can do something with these. Do you mind if I take them away?"

"Not at all. Be my guest."

"It's Friday. I can do it over the weekend. I'll have it ready for Monday."

"Fine, we'll run the experiment on Monday. I'll be interested to see what happens."

"Me too," I said. "Me too."

11

I had a pretty clear idea what was needed. Before I left the lab on Friday I shuffled through all the samples in that cupboard. When I left I had thirty-seven sheets, each one a different material but all the same size. The idea was to drop these, one at a time, into the space between the resonating beakers and see whether it had any effect. Obviously Rodge wasn't going to be standing inside the cage doing it by hand, and you can be bloody sure that I wasn't. So what I had to do was construct something very simple that we could control from outside.

I kept a few tools at the flat but not enough for this job so I decided to go home and use my Dad's. My folks don't usually go out on a Friday night, but I phoned my Mum just to check. Then I tossed the bare minimum into an overnight bag, made sure I had my old front door key and walked down to the Tube station at South Kensington.

The trains were packed with commuters at this time of day. I had to stand for a bit but it thinned out after Mile End. I got a seat and took out my notepad. By the time we'd reached Dagenham I had a rough drawing and a list of the materials I needed.

"Well, this is a nice surprise, Michael," Mum said, as she emerged from the kitchen, wiping her hands.

I gave her the usual peck on the cheek.

"How are you, Mum? All right?"

"Yes, love. You here for the weekend?"

"No, sorry—flying visit I'm afraid. I've got to go back to town tomorrow afternoon."

"Aah. Well, better than never. Tea's ready when you are."

We chatted a bit over tea. Mum asked me about the course and I said it was going okay. Of course I didn't say anything about the research or my little project.

After breakfast the following morning I followed Dad into the sitting room.

"Could I borrow the car, Dad? I need to go down the hardware store for a few odds and ends."

He didn't say anything, just dipped his hand into his trouser pocket and handed me the key to his small Rover.

"I'll have a bit of woodworking to do," I added. "I can do it in the garage. Okay if I use the tools? I'll oil them afterwards."

Dad always coats his tools with oil before he puts them away, to stop them rusting. If you forget to wipe them before you start it makes a hell of a mess of your hands—and the job.

"There's some bits of timber in there if you want to use 'em," he said.

I pictured that cobwebby corner of the garage, and suppressed a shudder.

"No, it's okay," I said airily. "I need some moulding and a length of beech dowel and stuff like that so I'll buy it all together."

Before long I was back from the shops and hard at work in the garage. I spent the rest of the morning sawing and drilling and loving every minute of it. Normally I busy myself a lot with my hands but ever since I'd joined that bloody M.Sc. course I'd done nothing but write essays and answer questions on test cases and learn international patent law and medical device regulations, and stuff like that. Now here I was, putting together an apparatus we were going to use for an experiment on Monday. I was like a dog with three tails.

I did everything but the glueing. I'd do that back at the flat so I could give it time to dry properly. I swept up the sawdust, oiled the tools and cleaned myself up. I looked at my watch. There was time to phone Suzy before lunch.

We had a nice chat. I found it easier to talk to her on the phone; maybe that was because we'd already broken the ice. I'd been trying to think of something we could do in the evening but the answer fell into my lap.

"Do you like the theatre, Mike?"

"Me? Oh yes, I love the theatre. I even love bad theatre."

"Well, I don't know about bad theatre…"

"No, I was only saying…"

"It's just that Siobhan and I—Siobhan's my flatmate—we had these tickets for a play, but she's gone down with an awful cold and she doesn't want to go anywhere now except bed. So would you like to go?"

I said, "That'd be great." Then as an afterthought, "As long as it's clearly understood that I pay my way."

She laughed at that, a teasing chuckle that made me go buzz-buzz inside.

"What's the play?"

I didn't give a damn but I thought I ought to ask.

"I don't know much about it because Siobhan booked it. I think it's set in post-war Germany. She says it's had very good reviews. It's on at Wyndham's. Shall we meet at the theatre? Seven o'clock?"

"Fine. I'll see you then."

I wasn't going to insist on picking her up if she didn't want me to.

*

I got there first. The foyer was packed with people all talking at the tops of their voices. Some were queuing to buy last-minute seats or programmes; others milled about or pushed past in a great waft of perfume or aftershave; and there was me, just trying to stand out of the way while I waited for her. I kept rising up on my toes to look this way and that but I needn't have worried: I spotted her the moment she walked in. She was wearing a green dress and she had a bit more make-up on than when I'd seen her after work and she looked absolutely stunning. She handed the tickets to me, which I thought was a nice thing to do, and we went inside. As we were going to our seats I saw several chaps look her way and then cast envious glances at me. I felt totally great.

It was a good play, very cleverly done. In the interval there was a real press of people at the bar so I bought ice creams instead. That went down well. Afterwards we walked down Shaftesbury Avenue and she said she knew a good place so we went there. I could have fancied a pint, actually, but the hot chocolate was very nice. We sat there discussing the play and the motives of the characters and the performances and the way it'd been staged. I thought she was really perceptive; she'd certainly noticed things that had gone right past me. I think we both felt pretty relaxed. Even so I had the feeling she was keeping her distance. That was okay; I was happy to let things develop at their own pace. We arranged to meet for a sandwich at lunchtime on Monday and parted company at Piccadilly Underground station. We didn't kiss but she gave my hand a squeeze and it seemed almost as good. I was ten feet tall again.

*

On Sunday morning I sat down at the kitchen table in my flat and stacked up the thirty-seven sheets of metal and plastic I'd taken from the laboratory. Then I took each sheet in turn and used a dob of epoxy to glue it into one of the grooves in my little apparatus. When it was finished it looked a bit like a toast rack, the toast being the sample sheets. Only the way I'd mounted them you could get any sample to swivel around one corner and come out of the stored position onto the table. I left the glue to set properly and after that I was at a bit of a loose end.

The rest of Sunday seemed to take for ever. I couldn't wait to see Suzy again. I kept thinking about how she'd looked when she arrived at the theatre and afterwards, when we were chatting over the hot chocolate, the way her eyes sparkled if I managed to come out with anything amusing, and the little tweaks of her mouth that made the dimples go deeper. The flat felt strangely empty and I found myself wandering around tending to things that didn't really need it. In the end I watched a lousy film on TV and went to bed.

12

Monday morning came and that dragged by as well, even though I was doing my best to concentrate on the tutorial. Finally it was lunchtime. I called for Suzy at the bank and we went to a place on Brompton Road where you can get a slice of pizza. I had to force myself to keep up a conversation; really and truly all I wanted was to be with her. I knew I was getting in deeper all the time but I just couldn't help it. More to the point, I didn't want to help it. Lunch hour went by in a flash and she had to go back to work. I had a couple of hours to finish my assignment for the day, with half my mind on Suzy and the other half on the experiment. It wasn't easy.

*

I made it over to Elec Eng at four o'clock. That dank cavern of a lab seemed almost welcoming now. My attention was on the cage and its equipment at the centre of the room and the dark recesses didn't even register with me any more.

I had my wooden contraption with the samples in a carrier bag and I produced it with a bit of a flourish. Rodge seemed well impressed. I dipped into the carrier bag again and pulled out a reel of forty-pound breaking strain monofilament nylon I'd bought at a fishing tackle shop in Dagenham. I looped a bit of nylon through a hole in the end of one of the mouldings to show him how it worked. I simply tugged sharply upwards on the nylon and the sample swivelled around and fell out onto the bench under its own weight. Then I tugged upwards again, enough to get it over top dead centre and back into the rack. Rodge promptly dubbed it "Mike's juke box", and actually that was a pretty good description.

It took me about an hour to rig it up properly in the cage, threading thirty-seven lengths of nylon and taking them through the copper mesh on the roof and over to the control panel area. I tied a spare piece of dowel to the roof of the cage to lift the nylon clear and stop it chafing against the mesh. To keep the lengths of nylon from springing back, I knotted them to heavy nuts and bolts. It was all a bit crude but it would only be for one experiment so it wasn't worth spending more time than that. I'd already numbered the ends of the pieces of moulding and written a key so as I'd know which sample was coming out of the rack at any one time.

All the time I was mucking about in and out of the cage Rodge wouldn't have any power going to any of the equipment. As soon as I'd finished he closed the cage door, went round to the other side and flipped the switches to turn on the power supplies. Then we went off to the corner of the lab for a cup of coffee while they stabilized.

"I've been thinking about the experiment," he said. "We need to ask ourselves what we're looking for, and how much of it has to occur before we see it, and how long that's going to take."

I looked at him steadily while something went down inside me like a lift. I was feeling a right clown. Here I was, all pleased with myself for making a bit of kit, and not really thinking it through properly, and Rodge had gone straight to the heart of the problem. It just underlined the difference between a top flight researcher like him and a barely competent one like me.

"I suppose I just thought the second object would disappear if the matter waves were absorbed," I volunteered.

"Well it's a completely symmetrical system so if anything both will disappear. Yes, you may be right. But suppose there's only a small amount of absorption? The mass will be removed gradually. Will we notice? You see, I haven't the first idea where the mass would disappear from first. Obviously if it came off the outside there wouldn't be a problem: we'd see it shrink or change shape. But what if it came out of every part of the object little by little? It would keep its structure right to the last moment. If it was made of metal or something like that, it would stay opaque until it was only a few atoms thick. Unless we let it go on for a long time we might not notice a thing. Hang on a moment."

He scribbled in a notebook, then turned it around to show me what he'd written.

$$M_n = M_0(1-a)^n$$

"Look at this, Mike. The system is actually very sensitive. You remember the coupled pendulum experiment? It takes several seconds for the swing to transfer from one pendulum to the other. Here a similar thing is happening but at about a hundred thousand times a second. Now what that means is that the matter waves pass back and forth through the material a great many times—in ten seconds it would be a million times. That's 'n' in the formula. In each pass a fraction of the total gets absorbed, I've called it 'a' in this formula. It only needs the material to be slightly absorptive and the mass is going to disappear fast. Let's do it on a spreadsheet."

He picked up a soft case from under the bench and unzipped it, drew out a laptop and booted it up. I stood behind him so that I could see the screen. He tapped in the formulae, dragged down some cells to get a time series, and then started trying it out with different values. He turned slightly to me, the side of his face outlined in the glow from the screen. I could see he was a bit excited, enjoying himself. Just like me building the apparatus.

"You see? If the absorption is one part in a million, there's only a hundredth of a percent left after ninety seconds. If the absorption is ten times higher," he entered "1.00E-5" into a cell on the spreadsheet, "well, much faster, you get there in a little over ten seconds."

"What about if it's ten times lower?"

He entered "1.00E-7".

"Ah, you see, totally different. After ninety seconds you'd still have over 40% left."

"So you're saying that if we watch it for a minute and a half we can be pretty sure to pick up any absorption more than one part in a million."

"That's exactly what I'm saying. Well, that's not bad, is it? It should be sensitive enough. Now the question is, what would be a good object to try it with?"

We both thought for a bit. Not a beaker of water, obviously. Nor a piece of cheese. You wanted something that wasn't the same all the way through, something that would change dramatically if it lost a bit of mass. I tried hard to think.

"I've got it," Rodge said suddenly. "What we need is a living organism!"

It was a brilliant idea, and I didn't like the sound of it at all.

"What," I said warily, "you mean like a rat?"

"Well, a rat would be ideal, but that's going to be hard to

get hold of at short notice. It doesn't have to be a mammal. We can use a spider. There are always some in that corner, where those spare bits of racking are."

He opened a drawer and took out a torch, picked up a glass tumbler from the side of the sink, tore the card front cover off his notebook, and then handed the whole lot to me.

"Here you are," he said cheerily. "You get a spider while I'm putting this lot away."

He'd powered down the laptop and was about to put it back in the case when he noticed that I hadn't moved.

"What's the matter?"

"Er, spiders aren't exactly my thing, Rodge. I mean I'm very glad the good Creator included them in the grand scheme of things and all that, but I'm just as happy not to be around them, if you know what I mean."

He looked at me with a sort of interested smile.

"All right."

He picked up the torch, tumbler and card and went over to the corner. When he came back there was one of the biggest, blackest spiders I've ever seen scrambling around on the card inside the inverted glass. I smiled queasily, doing my best to suppress the panic.

"Er, Rodge, all this energy isn't going to turn it into a ginormous one the size of a car, is it? Only I don't think I could hack that."

He grunted.

"You've been watching too many science fiction films. Get ready."

13

Rodge went into the cage and put the spider, still under the glass, on the table. I stayed outside; I wasn't going near it. He positioned it carefully, nodded his satisfaction and came out. I went round to the control panel. All the power supplies had stabilized, so as soon as Rodge had closed the cage door behind him I flicked on the charging circuits. Then I used the sliders to bring the radiated power up, just as I'd done before. He joined me and both of us looked intently into the cage. The spider had calmed down a bit now and it was wandering around the inside of the glass, exploring the limits of its new world. It still made my flesh crawl but I could take it as long as it stayed inside the glass. Fifteen seconds went by and the little rising choir of voices had flattened out; the capacitors were charged.

"Ready?" he said.

I glanced along the line of green and red lights. All present and correct.

"Yes," I replied.

I flicked off all the charging switches and placed my finger lightly on the red button.

"Go."

I pressed the red button and there was the usual clonk, and now there were two spiders inside two glasses. I was transfixed.

"All right," he said, "you can bring the radiated power

down now. It should be stable."

I did, and it was. We watched the spiders for a bit, and then I noticed something that made the hair prickle on my head.

"Hey, Rodge, did you see that? The one on the left moved, but the other one didn't."

We both watched for several minutes.

"You're right, they can move independently. I suppose that's reasonable, if you think about it. A passive object would have to produce two identical resonance images, but an active one might not. They could move differently as long as every part kept its relationship the same as in the original object. Interesting…"

I realized that my mouth was dry and my palms were sweaty. I rubbed them on my trousers. I was getting used to handling this powerful equipment, so I don't think it was the experiment that was making me so tense, it was more that damned spider—or spiders. I thought, *What does the world look like to you, spider, being in two places at once? It must be pretty confusing.* Thinking about that made me feel a bit better. The spider clearly had more problems than I did.

"Well," said Rodge, "shall we get on with it?"

"Oh, yes." What with the spiders and all, I'd got distracted. We were supposed to be testing the absorption of the materials with what Rodge called my juke-box. I could see now that he'd placed it very well. It was between the two glasses, but off to one side.

"What's first?" Rodge asked.

From where I was sitting I could see the reddish-brown sheen of the first sheet of material, but I checked the written key to be sure.

"Copper. 100%."

"All right. Whenever you're ready."

I tugged sharply at the nylon, but not hard enough. The sheet came up and dropped back again. I had another try and it almost worked. On the third go it went over top dead centre and flopped down right between the beakers. I almost forgot to look at my watch; we were going to give it a minute and a half. A minute and a half later the spider in the original position was still exploring the edges where the glass met the card on the table. The other spider was trying to climb up the walls of the glass. Obviously nothing was happening. I put a tick on my key next to copper, and looked questioningly at Rodge. He nodded.

I needed two tries to get the copper sheet back in place but I was beginning to get the hang of this.

"Aluminium next. Also 100%," I announced.

I managed to flick it over in one. Again it landed right between the glasses, and again a minute and a half went by without anything happening. So it went on. Methyl methacrylate, nickel-cobalt-chromium, magnesium alloy, galvanized steel, titanium. It was a strange collection of materials. I don't know what the old practical had been about, but I suppose it might have had something to do with corrosion resistance. PTFE, tungsten-chromium-vanadium steel, 360 stainless steel, brass, beryllium-copper, high-density polyethylene…

Nearly an hour and a half went by, and it wasn't so exciting any more. Nothing was happening, at least nothing that we could see. Rodge was getting bored too. He was half-sitting on the bench.

"We're already up to number thirty-five," I said. "Two more to go. I suppose we might as well finish the run."

"Yep, might as well. What's next?" he asked, without much interest.

I looked into the cage and back at the list.

"Molybdenum-coated steel," I said.

I jerked the sample into place with what was now a practised flick of the nylon. And suddenly Rodge was on his feet and I was all attention.

A wisp of steam or smoke had come off the sample sheet, and as I looked a circular patch in the middle started to glow red. The circle expanded, getting white hot in the middle, and then quite suddenly it all faded. The white turned to red and the red turned to black. I blinked my eyes. I couldn't see much because I had a whacking great after-image on my retina and wherever I looked it was still there drifting around in the centre of my vision. I could smell it, though; it reminded me of the time I'd helped a friend get his car repaired in a welding shop.

Gradually my sight returned to normal. Now I could see that there was a hole in the middle of the sample where it had melted right through. I looked for the glasses and the spiders, but there was no sign of them. And then I noticed that actually there was something: a few glistening greyish-white blobs where the first spider had been. They were tiny and the only reason I'd seen them was that the light was coming in that direction and happened to catch them. It struck me as odd. If the matter waves had been absorbed why was anything at all left behind? I was just about to mention it to Rodge, but he spoke first.

"Well, that was impressive, wasn't it? I didn't see when they disappeared but the whole thing lasted less than ten seconds, so we're certainly looking at more than one part in a hundred thousand absorption. Other steels didn't do it, so it must be the molybdenum. What do they use that for?"

"I was wondering about that myself. Molybdenum's very

hard and it's resistant to corrosion. I suppose they could use it as some sort of protective coating."

"Well it certainly makes a heck of a difference to the absorption. Put a tick by molybdenum, then. How many samples left, Mike?"

"Only one. But that sheet's pretty mangled. I'm not sure I can get it back into the rack."

"Well, it's not worth setting it all up again, is it? It wasn't a comprehensive test anyway. We've got the answer we wanted, which is that most materials don't absorb matter waves, but there are at least some that do."

I was looking at the copper sample on the end of the rack and then my eyes shifted to the copper mesh of the cage and a thought struck me.

"Rodge… would it work the other way round? I mean, if a material doesn't absorb the matter waves passing back and forth could you establish the resonance with a sheet of it actually in the way?"

He had a shocked, alert expression, and I knew he'd latched on. I continued:

"I mean, we know now that copper doesn't absorb, so if that was true I suppose you could establish the resonant image, or whatever you call it, *outside* the cage."

A slow smile was spreading over his face.

"Yes," he said slowly. "I can't see why not…" He looked at me, and there was something new in his eyes. "That's a great idea, Mike! We should try it." He sized up the distance. "About 10 feet. Assuming a linear relationship, we need about five times the dollop of energy. That's easy, there's loads of reserve. We can increase the voltage or the duration. Duration's the easiest. I just have to replace the timing capacitor in the driver to the relay. It won't take long. You could take your bits and pieces out of the cage while I'm doing it. Let's power down."

So while I was cutting the ends off thirty-seven lengths of nylon and pulling them back into the cage, and unstrapping the dowel from the roof of the cage, and generally tidying things up, he was working inside the cabinet that housed the relay. I was beginning to flag a bit now; it had been a long day. But Rodge was all fired up and it had been my suggestion, after all, so I couldn't very well say, "Cheerio, I'm off."

After a bit he closed and latched the cabinet door and straightened up.

"Right. I'll go and find another glass and another spider," he said.

I was on the point of saying, "Does it have to be a spider, Rodge?" when I managed to stop myself; I didn't want to sound like a wimp. All the same I was hoping he'd be content with a nice small one. I knew it was a pretty forlorn hope and, sure enough, the one he came back with was even bigger and hairier than the first. It was frantically climbing up the inside of the glass, dropping off, and climbing up again. I bit my lip and kept well clear. If he noticed, he didn't comment. He set it all up on the table as before, but without the juke-box, of course.

In fact the juke-box was on the bench outside now, so we switched on the power supplies and while they were stabilizing we had a closer look at the melted sample. The hole was a couple of inches across. Rodge put his finger in the hole and ran it around the edges.

"It's completely smooth," he said. "Look, the steel's melted back over the edges. But there's nothing like enough there to account for the size of that hole. Some of it must have vaporized."

"Bloody hell. It must have got incredibly hot, incredibly fast."

"Yes. It must have."

We took up our positions.

"Same procedure as before, Mike. The circuit breaker will probably sound different, but that's about all you'll notice."

I nodded and went through the motions. I was concentrating hard, trying not to think about that spider, which was still climbing up and sliding down inside the glass. When everything was set I looked up at Rodge and he nodded and I pressed the red button. The relay went *ker-lonk*, and almost simultaneously there was a mighty crash of breaking glass. I nearly jumped out of my skin—and then I went rigid. The floor outside the end of the cage was littered with broken glass and that huge spider was running across the floor. I opened my mouth but no sound came out. It was like one of those awful dreams where you're trying to escape but you're running up a pile of loose sand, your feet are sliding back and you're not going anywhere. Somewhere in the distance I could hear Rodge's voice saying, "Mike, just detune and bring the power down… Mike!" Then he pushed me out of the way and swivelled the big knob and pulled back on the sliders and suddenly all the glass was gone, and the spider with it. It had tidied up like something out of *The Sorcerer's Apprentice.* And I was Mickey Mouse.

I swallowed with difficulty and did my best to get my voice under control.

"Sorry, Rodge. Sorry. I should have put something outside the cage—a table or something—for it to project onto. Didn't think of it."

I couldn't look at him. My nerves were still screaming.

"No problem," he dismissed my apology. "Even when the

glass was in pieces each part kept its relationship to the original. It was just a matter of killing the resonance."

I looked inside the cage. The spider was there, inside the glass, still climbing up and dropping down as if nothing had happened, as if it, or some resonant echo of it, hadn't just been making a bid for freedom across the floor of the lab. I took a deep breath, and then the implications of what we had just done crashed in on me. I looked at Rodge and he looked at me. I could see from his face that the same thought had occurred to him.

If you can do that with a spider, then why not with a mouse? And if with a mouse, why not with a man? And if you can set up a resonant image of yourself ten feet away on the other side of the copper mesh wall of a cage, then why not forty feet away, on the other side of the wall of this building? Or a hundred feet? Or a mile?

At that moment I wondered how long it would be before it was Rodge sitting in that cage waiting for me to press the big red button.

14

Soon after that Rodge came to live in my flat. The way it happened was this. I got over to the lab that day at about three-thirty. True, it was a bit earlier than usual, but not by much. Rodge wasn't there so I carried on with the modifications we were making to the equipment. If we were going to project resonating objects to different distances we needed much finer control of the dollop of energy. We decided to adjust the voltage in a series of precise steps. Within each step we'd get fine adjustment by controlling the pulse duration digitally. That way we could set any energy level throughout the range with great precision. I'm pretty handy with digital circuit design, so that part was my job.

Rodge came in about half an hour later. He was white with anger and he kept walking this way and that running his hand through his hair and hissing, "Bastard, bastard…" It took me completely by surprise. I was still holding the soldering iron, poised over the circuit board.

"What's the matter, Rodge? Where have you been?"

He looked at me for a moment, then sat heavily on a stool at the bench where I was working.

"I've been to see my bank manager—" his lip curled as he added, "—at his invitation. He read me the riot act. I know the overdraft has got too large, I know that. But it's only a matter of time before I start to pay it off. He won't wait any longer. He's ready to send the bailiffs in. Says he's warned me countless times and his patience is at an end. God, he's obnoxious! You know," he laughed derisively, "he kept saying 'Sir', but he treated me like something the dog left on the carpet."

I knew that would bug Rodge even more than the threat of legal action.

"Hell. What are you going to do?"

"I don't know. I mean, God knows I don't live extravagantly. But I've got to pay rent and put bread on the table."

He put his elbows on the bench and buried his head in his hands. He was usually so controlled. I hated to see him like this. I thought quickly.

"Look, Rodge. Why don't you give up your flat and come in with me? My place isn't large but we could manage. At least there'd only be one lot of rent to pay. We can come to some arrangement about the food. You know, just while you're going through this difficult patch."

He looked up at me slowly. There was a look of distant hope in his eyes.

"Really, Mike? It would solve a lot of problems. Are you sure you don't mind?"

I stuck the soldering iron back in its stand and switched it off.

"We'll leave this for now. Come on, we'll do it right now. I'll help you shift your gear."

You could say that was my first big mistake. At the time it seemed like the right thing to do.

*

Although it was busy in the lab—and remember, I was still trying to keep up with the M.Sc. course—I saw Suzy as much as I could. Usually we'd meet up at lunchtime and have a pizza or a sandwich together. At the weekend we'd take in a film or go to a restaurant or a club. The trouble was, it wasn't going any further than that. We seemed to enjoy each other's company—well, I was certainly enjoying hers. And I admit I was also enjoying the envious stares of other blokes as we walked along the street; nothing surprising there because she is good-looking, and no question. I could sense there was some sort of problem, though, and eventually I found out what it was. As I recall, it was a Saturday evening, and we were having a coffee after going to the cinema.

"It's nice to be getting out again," she said. "You know, Mike, I'd cut myself off socially before you came along."

"Why on earth would you do a thing like that?"

"Oh, I'd been going out with this fellow—we'd been together a long time. Then suddenly it all got unpleasant and ended. I was very upset—I don't really want to talk about it. To be honest, I still feel pretty bruised. I know it's all over with him, but these things take time. I hope you don't mind, Mike. You know, just taking things slowly the way we are?"

"No, sure, I understand."

She put a hand over mine and gave it a little squeeze.

"You're very kind, Mike. You know, I feel really comfortable with you."

I felt a bit better about it, now that I knew what the problem was. If she wanted to take things gradually it was all right with me; I liked her far too much to want to rush in and spoil things. I can be as patient as a cat waiting by a mouse-hole if I want to be. My main worry was that it would start to get platonic. I mean, I was glad she felt comfortable with me but I wanted more from our relationship than that. And then there was the way she'd kiss me goodnight. She'd bob up and peck me affectionately and run off. I had this urge to cup my hand around the nape of her lovely neck and bury myself in those full lips. Instead I'd be left standing there, running my tongue over my lips, savouring the taste of her lipstick. My chest ached with longing for her. I fantasized about her pressing that shapely body hard against me. But if she needed more time, what could I say? I was suffering, yet happy to be suffering. All a bit weird, really.

Now that she trusted me, I thought it might help if I invited her round to the flat. I offered to cook dinner and she agreed to come. I told her it wouldn't be anything fancy, and it wasn't, but I did my best to present it nicely. I already knew she liked New Zealand Sauvignon Blanc so I bought a bottle and planned the meal round that. We had avocado for starters with a raspberry vinaigrette. Then I served up farfalle with smoked salmon and a side salad. My pastas are pretty good, even though I say so myself, and she really enjoyed it. I'm not into desserts so I just did a fruit salad with some ice-cream. That suited her fine, because she isn't a big eater. We were just finishing dessert when Rodge came back from the lab. I introduced them and Rodge kind of nodded hello, much the same way he'd done to me when I first walked in on him about a month ago.

"Do you want something to eat, Rodge?" I offered. "There's another avocado in the bowl, and there's some smoked salmon left over."

"No thanks, I ate on the way home," he said.

"Glass of wine, then?"

"Yes, all right."

We chatted a bit and then Rodge went off to the lounge, leaving Suzy and me together in the kitchen. He said he had some calculations to work through. I thought he hadn't gone out of his way to be nice to Suzy, but she didn't seem to mind. In any case, she said, it was time she was getting back. We called a cab; she wouldn't let me take her home. She thanked me a lot for the dinner and said how delicious everything had been and she knew I'd gone to a lot of trouble and it was really sweet of me. The peck she gave me was fractionally longer than before.

15

Rodge and I were doing a lot of experiments now, using the new, precise control we had over energy. We used ordinary objects—there was no need to use spiders, thank God. We projected the resonating object up to twenty feet, but that was all we could manage inside the lab. Over those distances it seemed to be proportional to power—if you doubled the power, you doubled the distance—but they were short distances, so you couldn't really tell for sure. To make progress we needed to project much further. We knew we could project through the wall because we'd tried it. The trouble was, the object disappeared; we hadn't the first clue where it had landed up. It could be on the other side of the wall or half a mile away for all we knew.

Eventually Rodge said, "There's only one way to do this."

"What's that?"

"I have to get in the cage. If I'm projected I'll know exactly where I am, and we can measure it up afterwards."

Well, I was half-expecting it, like I said before, but I was still a bit taken aback.

"That's a bit drastic, isn't it? Is it safe?"

"Well of course it isn't safe. It's bloody dangerous. Mind you, the spider seemed all right, but then it's a pretty low life-form."

I could say amen to that.

"I'll get in touch with Tom Mayhew again. I think he's

still at Queen's. See if he can lend us a rat."

Obviously Rodge wasn't going to tell Tom Mayhew what we were really up to or say anything about his plans to go inside the cage himself. So he said it was an extension of what they'd done when they were working together before, with a mixture of different wavelengths applied simultaneously. That was fairly near to the truth. It was totally illegal, of course, because we weren't licensed to work with animals, but eventually Tom agreed to help us out provided his rat wasn't harmed and he could return it to the colony afterwards. Of course we couldn't guarantee that but we gave him what assurances we could. In the end he really came up with the goods: he brought us a rat he'd trained. It had learned a maze and how to get food by responding to different signals in some sort of apparatus. Afterwards he'd be able to check its behaviour and see if it remembered the tasks. As a test subject it couldn't have been better.

We did short projections at first, just a couple of feet. The rat became two rats and looked a bit startled; then the two of them went back to what they were doing. As we'd noticed with the spiders, they would sometimes do different things, like one would clean its whiskers while the other one was eating. I'd found that surprising enough with the spider, but I can tell you, when it happens with an animal like a rat it looks even more odd. After each experiment we'd bring the two back together, and watch it carefully for a while. In the end we took the plunge and did a projection through the copper mesh and over to a table we'd placed about twenty feet away, on the other side of the room. The rat wasn't running around there because we projected its cage with it; we weren't taking any chances. Then we detuned and powered down and the two rats became one. Again we looked carefully, but again the animal seemed none the worse for having led a dual existence. Rodge put the rat, still in its cage, into a sports bag and took a cab round to Queen's to return it to Tom.

We stayed at my flat the next day, waiting for Tom to call us. We knew the result was going to be crucial and neither of us could settle down to anything. Rodge fiddled around with some calculations. I tried to study a course text, but it was hopeless: I'd turn a page and wonder what I'd read on the previous one. Our nerves were stretched taut. When the phone finally rang at five o'clock we both jumped. Rodge took the call.

"Hi, Tom. Yes. Right, so you've been testing it all day…"

I realized he was repeating the conversation for my benefit.

"Behaviourally normal, total retention of memory, normal problem-solving abilities. Does that mean it's okay? Oh good. Thanks a lot, Tom. We really appreciate your help."

That was it. It seemed the way was clear.

*

Three weeks is all it took. Three weeks between the crucial experiment with the spider, when the full possibilities started to dawn on us, and Rodge sitting in a chair inside the cage with me charging the capacitors and bringing up the radiated power. And then waiting, my finger poised over the big red button.

RODGER

16

I was getting along perfectly well on my own and if Mike hadn't happened along that's the way I'd have kept it. When it comes to work I find most people very irritating. They swan through life without an original thought in their heads, and then—like Ledsham—fully expect to take credit for what you've done, just because they happen to be around at the time. They even steal your ideas and publish them as their own, so you've got to be careful. There are exceptions, of course. Tom Mayhew was one. Mike was another.

I didn't mind working with Mike and it didn't annoy me to have him around. It was the same in our undergraduate days. Some people thought we were an unlikely pair, because he was in no way my intellectual equal. Actually—setting aside for the moment that I didn't care a damn what they thought or said—they were completely missing the point. I know he was inordinately grateful to me for explaining the things to him that he couldn't understand, but it wasn't pure altruism. Mike was actually quite useful to me, as a sort of litmus test of my own understanding. If I could explain something to him in a way he could grasp then I knew I'd mastered it properly myself. If I couldn't explain it, I'd say to him, "Sorry, Mike, I need to clarify this a bit in my own mind." I didn't try to fob him off with a lot of jargon and I didn't sneer at his limited intellectual ability, as some people might have done. Because it was like a flag being waved, telling me that my own understanding was incomplete. And that would prompt me to go into it in much greater depth, until I did understand it properly. Then we would sit down together and I would explain it to him again.

I suppose he was a bit of a puppy dog at college, following me around as he did, but it didn't do any harm. The good thing about Mike is that he's uncomplicated; you know where you are with him, you never feel there's a hidden agenda. I couldn't say that for the rest of them. Mike was certainly no idiot, but he was no genius either; his great virtue was to know his limitations and be honest about them. The others all thought they were better than they actually were. It's true that some of them were academically able, but they didn't have any real vision. As far as the physics course was concerned, they could only see as far as passing the exams and getting well-remunerated jobs; that was the extent of their love of science. And because they didn't feel the need to acquire any deeper insight they missed the point about Mike and myself, which was that our relationship was as valuable to me as it was to him. It was fortuitous that we were able to pick it up again several years later when he came back to the University to do his M.Sc.. By then he was reasonably competent technically, so he could be quite helpful around the lab.

It must have come as a surprise to him to discover how deep in debt I was. He would have assumed I was properly funded as a postdoctoral fellow, and up to that point I hadn't disabused him of the notion. In actual fact I wasn't receiving any funding at all. It was no fault of mine. I knew I'd made a damned good job of my doctoral research, and my so-called supervisor, Ledsham, had to acknowledge that. He disliked me, all the same—I know he did. Perhaps he felt a twinge of guilt because he'd made no intellectual contribution to the work whatsoever—not even to the joint paper Tom and I had put his name on. You'd have thought he'd have been grateful to have something to put in his report to the electricity company, to show them they'd got something of value for their money. But when I approached him about a postdoctoral appointment he was totally unhelpful.

"I don't think that's on, Rodger," he said. "I'll be continuing as Dean for the moment, so I'm not going to have any time to run a research lab. I don't have any funding for a postdoc and because of my commitments I can't in all conscience apply for it."

"What about a lectureship?"

"Out of the question. There aren't any vacancies, and even if there were you're far too inexperienced. No, my advice to you would be to broaden your experience elsewhere. That's the usual career pattern, you know. You're a capable chap. You should be able to find another lab to take you on."

It wasn't what I wanted to hear. It might be the usual strategy to move around and gain experience in different labs, but I wasn't looking for a conventional career. If I moved I'd have to work for someone else on what they fondly believed to be a worthwhile project, knowing all the time that I had a far more ambitious goal that was very nearly within my grasp. I knew exactly what I wanted to do, and I was well equipped to do it. The windowless old lab, with its damp walls and peeling paint, had an excellent power supply. Then there was all the apparatus I'd been putting together over the last three years; I couldn't leave all that behind.

"Prof, I'm sure that's good advice," I told him, "but the thing is, my doctoral work here has opened up a number of avenues which I'm very keen to explore. I don't actually need anything further in the way of equipment or running costs. How would it be if I stayed on, on a purely honorary basis?"

"Well, that would be most unusual. I suppose if you think you can manage I can't object. We're already short of space in the School but I don't think there'll be any great demand for that lab you're occupying until it's properly refurbished. I have to say again I can't offer you a salary, but I'll do what I can to arrange an ex gratia payment out of college funds. Perhaps you can do some paid demonstrating in undergraduate practical classes—that might help you make ends meet. But I do urge you to think of this as a temporary measure. It would be far better, from a career point of view, if you got a properly funded postdoctoral position somewhere else."

That was all I wanted. After that conversation I didn't see him again. He did get me the ex gratia payment but it was hardly worth having. I never followed up on the demonstrating and I have no intention of doing so now. I had quite enough of students when I was an undergraduate myself.

My debts started to mount up, of course, but there was no way I was going to ask mother for help. If you want to know why, you have to know a little about my background. Mother was a Laverne-Villiers; they can trace their family back to the twelfth century. But as with a lot of the old families, death duties had taken their toll, the houses needed a lot of upkeep, and the money was running out. Mother was very handsome—well, she still is. She caught the eye of Dukas at some reception or other, and he started to pay her a lot of attention. He was very much new money: investment banking, mergers and acquisitions, that sort of thing. The family were enthusiastic about the match—because of the money, of course. I think he was keen because he thought it would give him an entrée into polite society. I don't know whether mother was attracted to him, or even liked him, but she was always a strong believer in duty. So the marriage went ahead. Incidentally, I got all this from a talkative old aunt. Mother would never have confided anything like that in me; she bore her lot with fortitude and totally in private.

It was a big wedding with a lot of publicity, but once they were married things failed to go according to plan. On the one side, the family declined to admit him to their own circle, let alone introduce him into society. To be fair I think they did try a small dinner party or two but he was just an embarrassment to them; he was too loud and uncouth for their refined company. On the other side, the expected largesse from Dukas showed no sign whatsoever of materializing. He took no interest in the upkeep of the main part of the estate. He didn't even want to live there. He was abroad most of the time, on business, as he liked to put it. He installed mother in a modest house on the estate—I think it once belonged to a gamekeeper—and gave her some sort of allowance, but I know it wasn't nearly enough to live on. He probably spent more on his other women in a week than he gave her in a month. Fortunately her uncle was old Lord Rambourne. He was fond of her, and as he didn't have any family of his own he left her a bequest. After he died it kept her going, particularly as she now had a son to bring up. I believe mother named me after one of my illustrious forebears, Sir Rodger de Villiers. It didn't make any difference to me. Names aren't important; you are who you are.

So now I was part of the Dukas household, but it didn't take long for me to realize that I didn't feature importantly in father's grand design. He didn't ill-treat me: he just ignored me. It was like I wasn't there. He'd come home for a few days and spend most of it going at my mother. And not just in the bedroom either. I remember one occasion—I suppose I was about eight—when I went down to the kitchen in my pyjamas to get a drink of water. Mother was standing at the sink doing the washing-up. He'd come up, lifted her skirt and pulled down her panties, and he was having her from behind, holding her strongly by the hips and bending and straightening his knees to get a good thrust. And she just stood there quietly, head hung forward, waiting for him to finish, her rubber-gloved hands extended to either side of the sink to steady herself, the soap bubbles popping as they dried on her gloves. I crept away without them seeing me, feeling revolted and at the same time strangely excited. It was an image that returned to me again and again. After a while he started to come to the house less and less frequently. I had few regrets about that, and I'm sure Mother felt the same way.

You might have thought that, with an animal like that for a husband and father, mother and I would have grown closer together, but it didn't work like that. I don't know why. Perhaps she thought the marriage would have been more successful if I hadn't come along, although that was fairly hard to believe. Perhaps she resented me because I got in the way of her marrying someone else, someone more cultivated. I'm sure it hurt her the way father ignored me, and no doubt she would have liked me to achieve something spectacular, just to get back at him. I'm afraid I failed her in that respect. I didn't need him or care what he thought about me, and I wasn't going to be a pawn in their game. I went to a good public school and did moderately well but not brilliantly. The school was keen for me to sit the entrance exams for

Cambridge but I got impatient with the stupid questions they asked me at interview and that didn't go down too well. I wasn't bothered when they failed to give me a place. I was already interested in the physics of matter and it seemed to me that Prince Albert had the better course anyway.

When I was an undergrad I used to go home during the long vacations, but the family didn't share my interest in science; their interest was limited to my potential earning power. Mother expressed no opinion one way or the other. I got a First, but only because I wanted to be able to compete successfully for a research studentship. I decided not to give my mother or my absentee father the satisfaction of seeing the degree awarded; at the time of the degree ceremony I arranged to be on holiday in France. I haven't been home since I got the Ph.D. There's no way I could approach her for money now, even if I thought she had it to give me. For the moment, then, I've had to let the debts mount up.

The bank manager who was around when we first came to the University was a decent chap who took a long view. He knew we were all bright enough to earn a good living, and that some of us would be high-fliers, financially speaking. So he regarded my custom as a long-term investment, and the growing debt a temporary aberration that would be corrected in good time. The new manager, Mr. Meredrew, has a less charitable outlook. Although he's constrained not to voice his opinions, it's fairly obvious that so far as he's concerned students are a lot of free-loaders cluttering up his nice bank, and the sooner he can be shot of us, and have some decent clients' assets to play with, the happier he'll be. In fact I don't think happiness even enters into the equation for Meredrew. Since nothing can ever live up to his standards, what other people would experience as happiness he regards merely as a lesser degree of irritation.

The last time he called me in, he was really offensive about my overdraft. He sat there in his grey suit and carefully ironed striped shirt with the white collar and tightly knotted tie and matching pocket handkerchief, and in his condescending manner and disdainful voice proceeded to tell me my responsibilities, and spelt out all the legal consequences for me in great detail and, I thought, with a certain relish. I despised him more than anyone I have ever met. It took a real effort of self control not to put my fist in his face there and then, and I was still choking on my own bile when I got back to the lab.

17

Mike, to his credit, didn't try to probe into the reasons for my lack of solvency. He saw the state I was in and suggested straight away that I moved into his flat. That's typical of Mike; he sees what needs to be done and he does it. I must say it was a mighty relief because I was behind on the rent and with Meredrew foreclosing on me I hardly knew what to do next.

I'd rented furnished accommodation so there wasn't much stuff to move; it was mostly clothes, and I don't have a large wardrobe. As soon as we got back to his flat, Mike took charge of the situation. He cleared a few drawers for me, gave me some hanging space for jackets and trousers, and then came in with an armful of bedclothes.

"Here are some blankets and spare sheets. This sofa converts to a bed—I'll show you how. You'll need to strip the bed every morning and put the sheets and blankets in here," he indicated a drawer, "so we can use the room as a lounge again. You can make the bed up again in the evening. It's not a problem if you want an early night because I mostly do my work on the kitchen table."

"I really appreciate this, Mike."

"That's okay. It's not a permanent solution but it makes sense until you're back on your feet. Can you cook?"

"I know several different ways of preparing eggs. But I'm afraid that's the limit of my…"

"All right, it's not a problem. I can do the cooking."

He continued to show me round the flat while he explained how we could divide the tasks. It was as if he was ticking off the items on a mental list: cooking, washing-up, shopping, laundry, housework... I was in no position to argue—after all, he was putting a roof over my head—but I did find myself wondering whether it was really necessary to have this degree of organization. Somehow I'd muddled along before without devoting so much of my precious time to the minutiae of day-to-day living. The thought occurred to me that he might entertain people here from time to time. The whole place was so neat and clean that you could have invited anyone back at zero notice. That's not something you could have said for my place, but then I didn't do any entertaining so the problem didn't arise. Well, if he did have visitors I supposed I'd be meeting them soon enough.

*

By now Mike had become very familiar with the equipment, so I could feel reasonably confident when I took my place in the cage with him at the control panel. If something did go wrong, I felt he'd know what to do. But I was determined that nothing would go wrong. I spent the whole of the previous day checking the tuning and output of every generator, every amplifier, every photodiode array, every laser. I took the table out of the cage to make room for a chair under the antenna array. And before I even went into the cage I had the power supplies running for an hour, and checked once again that everything was within spec. It was, so I went and sat in the chair and he started to charge the capacitor bank and run up the radiated power.

"Mike? After we've projected, wait for a bit. I'll raise my hand when I want you to kill the resonance. When that happens, detune and power down, all right? If I don't raise my hand in two minutes, do it anyway."

"Okay. Are you still sure about this, Rodge?"

"Yes, yes, quite sure. Let's do it."

"Okay, I'm pressing the button…now!"

I heard the circuit breaker go clonk and I had a brief sensation of movement, a bit like the feeling you have when you get off a boat and the ground still seems to be heaving. I realized I must have been projected but I couldn't interpret my sensations. The main problem was my vision; it seemed confused, doubled. I persevered for a bit, then made a decision and raised my hand. There was a pause and then suddenly things returned to normal. Mike sounded very anxious.

"Are you all right, Rodge? It worked, you know. It was weird. There were two of you! What did it feel like?"

I stood up and opened the door to join him outside the cage.

"Look, Mike, can we talk about it in a moment? I need to do it again, but further this time—out of the cage and into the lab. It's just too difficult inside the cage: the visuals from the two positions are overlapping and it's terribly confusing. If I could get a completely different viewpoint I'd be able to make a better assessment."

He looked a bit chagrined that I wasn't more forthcoming, but it really wasn't easy to put into words at this stage. I took a tape-measure out of a drawer and gave it to Mike to hold. He stood with it, next to the cage, and I stretched it out to the point in the room I wanted him to project me to. The distance was six metres. I squatted on my heels briefly to get a rough idea of what I'd see from the new position and fixed that in my mind. Then I retracted the tape-measure.

"Okay, Mike. Bring up the volts on that "–OH" power supply now, to give it a chance to settle."

He went over to the control panel while I got out my laptop. I put up the graph of distance against energy and started to calculate the new settings.

Mike said, "Right, done that. What about the dollop?"

"I'm just doing it… all right, got it now. First notch on the voltage, and set the duration to three hundred and sixty milliseconds."

"Gotcha."

Mike busied himself making the necessary adjustments and I went back into the cage and took up my position on the chair. I didn't have to face ahead, or anything like that, so I watched his movements. I saw him flip the lever switches for the capacitors, heard the multiple whine as they charged up. Then he went over to the slider controls and brought up the power again. He checked the lights and flipped back the lever switches to stop the capacitors charging.

"All set here, Rodge."

"Right. Same again, Mike. I'll signal if I want you to stop the resonance. Otherwise keep it going for two minutes and then stop it anyway."

"Understood."

I gave him a thumbs-up to show I was ready.

"Here we go, then."

The circuit breaker went clonk.

Straight away I knew something had gone wrong.

18

I'd assembled a picture in my mind of what to expect, but when the circuit breaker went clonk it wasn't at all the way I'd imagined. I could feel a breeze on my face and cool air tingling in my nostrils, and I was aware of grass all around me. I must have panicked, because my heart was hammering in my ears. I had to force myself to think rationally.

The settings must have been wrong, that much was clear. I hadn't thought we could be that far out, but perhaps there was something I'd overlooked. Maybe there was a mass dependence in the equation—after all, I was a lot heavier than anything we'd used before.

My first worry was how Mike would react when he saw I hadn't projected inside the room. He'd see only one of me, so he might think it hadn't worked. But he was probably smart enough to realize I'd projected too far. If he was over-anxious he'd detune and power down straight away. If he kept his head, he'd keep looking out for my signal and waiting for the time to elapse. Either way, I told myself, I'd be back in the cage inside two minutes, so I might as well relax.

Feeling calmer, I started to take a closer interest in my sensations.

The visual impressions were the most confusing. I was looking across a grassy area towards some trees. Behind the trees there was a street and beyond that some tall buildings. The message was "You're in the open air", yet at the same time I had the conflicting sensation of being enclosed, of shadows and angular shapes over and around me. I realized my brain was trying to reconcile two different views: the view from wherever I'd been projected to, and the view I still had of the inside of the cage. It was like pausing to look into the interior of a shop when the window is reflecting things going on in the street behind you. In that situation, if you concentrate hard you can shut out the reflections and start to see into the shop, whereas if you concentrate on the reflections of people walking by on the pavement and cars in the road you become less aware of the inside of the shop. By using that technique and concentrating hard I gradually suppressed more and more the angular shadows and the claustrophobic feelings that went with them. As I did so the open-air scene became sharper and more real. I looked around me.

I was in a square, one of those oases of green you find all over central London. That much was obvious, but which one? It looked vaguely familiar but to find out I'd have to cross over to the corner of the street beyond the trees so that I could read the street name. Something inside was telling me to get on with it, but I couldn't move. I had this overpowering feeling that I had to stay glued to the chair in case Mike returned it and me to the cage. The sensible thing, I thought, would be to take it in easy stages, and try a walkabout next time. But then I thought: *How can you be sure there's going to be a second time? You don't know what happened to get you out here this time. It might have been a freak combination that you can't repeat.* I recalled the incident with the spider and the shattered glass and told myself firmly that it didn't matter how far I wandered from the chair; as soon as the resonance was broken, both the chair and I would return to our related points inside the cage. All the same, I hadn't entirely convinced myself. These distances were much greater than anything we'd tried in the lab. Suppose I was wrong and suppose I was on the other side of the square when the two minutes were up? Two minutes! I'd forgotten to look at my watch when Mike pressed the button! How much time had I spent just sitting here and thinking about it? Thirty seconds? It could be a lot longer—I really had no idea. I took a deep breath. Enough of this faffing around. *Do it.*

I couldn't just get up and walk; I had to be really sure that my counterpart in the cage didn't get up and walk at the same time. Otherwise he could bump into something and hurt himself; more importantly, he could move outside the coverage of the antenna array, and that could be really serious. So I started by studying the ground under my feet. The grass was still shifting and alternating with the floor of the cage. I concentrated on the grass until that became stable. Then I let my awareness extend from the grass to my feet, and from my feet to my legs, focusing on the sensations that told me that my legs were connected to my feet, and that my feet were planted firmly on the grass. Then I simply stood up. I was fairly sure that the movement had been confined to my projected body. I now felt quite anchored in the new environment; almost nothing remained to me of the cage. I walked quickly over to the corner of the square and read the enamelled plaque on the corner building. Innisfree Square. Of course! It was just on the other side of Museum Road; I'd once visited an acquaintance in a hall of residence here.

Suddenly everything swam and I was back in the cage, sitting on the chair. The angular frame of the cage, which had haunted my vision moments earlier, was now sharp and solid all around me. There was a distant clamouring that quickly got louder. It was a voice, Mike's voice.

"Rodge! Rodge? Are you okay? Are you all right?"

Was I all right? It seemed I was. Feelings of exhilaration and relief started to well up inside me. I'd been on the other side of the square when he'd returned me, but here I was, in the cage again, sitting on the chair! It had worked!

"I'm fine, Mike. Don't worry. I'm all right."

"Are you sure? Jeez, that was the longest two minutes of my life. First off I thought nothing had happened. There were supposed to be two of you, one in the cage and one over there, but all I could see was the one in the cage. Then you didn't get up or anything so I figured it must have worked after all. Where on earth did you disappear to?"

I tried to sound nonchalant.

"Actually I've been outside, enjoying the fresh air."

He looked at me and blinked.

"You went through the cage and the wall of the building? Bloody hell! Are you sure you're all right?"

"Yes, yes, I told you, I'm fine."

He had the cage door open. I got up a little unsteadily and followed him out.

"Look," I said, "shall we just check the settings before we go any further?"

The moment we did I saw what had gone wrong. The duration was set correctly but the voltage was on the second step, not the first. I pointed to it. Realization dawned on Mike's face.

"You said 'first notch on the voltage'. I thought you meant first click up! Oh God, I'm sorry."

"It's my fault. I should have made myself clearer. Well, no harm done. In fact, it's put us way ahead of the game. You did well to wait out the two minutes, Mike. It's just lucky I didn't end up in the middle of Kensington High Street."

His eyebrows flicked up as he took the point. Then he looked thoughtful.

"Suppose you had, and a car knocked you down and killed you. Would you be still be okay when we returned you to the cage?"

"Well, I suppose if it was only physical damage, yes. If there was a great shard of metal stuck through me I... look, why are we discussing this? We have to see to it that it won't happen. We have to be much more precise in future. We need to be able to predict just how far I'm projected at any given power setting."

"So where exactly did you end up? Do you know?"

"Yes. Innisfree Square."

"That's... what, half a mile away?'

"Less. We need a large scale map so we can measure it. I wish we could be more precise—I'm not even sure within twenty metres whereabouts in the Square I landed."

For a moment both of us were lost in thought. We needed a way of measuring those distances more accurately. Mike came up with the answer, and it was so obvious I don't know why I didn't think of it first.

"GPS!" he exclaimed. "A quality handheld global positioning system receiver. The new ones are good to a metre. Blackstones in Fulham would have them—you know, the camping, expedition, and mountaineering place. Shouldn't set us back too much. Don't worry," he added, seeing the expression on my face, "I'll lay out."

There wasn't any point in doing more experiments until we'd got that sorted, so we powered down the equipment and went back to his flat. He wanted to know in great detail everything I'd experienced. I did my best to describe it to him, but of course it wasn't easy to convey something like that. Still, he could share my excitement. We'd taken a big leap forward. We'd planned to take it step by step: showing I could be projected without ill effects, showing I could be projected through the wall, again without ill effects, and showing I could move around at the other end and still be brought back to the cage as before. And we'd done all three in one fell swoop.

Mike had a tutorial next morning but he went down to Fulham straight after that and came back to the lab with a couple of plastic carrier bags. He was beaming all over his face as he showed me what he'd bought.

In the first carrier bag was a box containing a portable GPS receiver.

"It's the most accurate model they stock," he enthused, as he removed it from its packing. "The guy in the shop gave me the de luxe tour. It's stacked with features. What really sold it to me is the built-in memory. It means you don't have to note down readings: you can just store them. There's an electronic compass, too. I suppose we won't need that, though."

"No. If we want to, we can work out the direction from the reading we take outside and the reading in the cage. As well as the distance, of course."

"Ah, distance. Now, look at this."

He opened the other carrier bag and took out a colourful cardboard box.

"Ta-dah!" he sang triumphantly. "Software. This is a pretty versatile package. Pilots use it for navigation. And..."

He delved into the bag and came out with a map.

"I went to the stationers on the High Street. It's the largest scale sheet map of London I could find."

"Excellent, Mike. Well done!"

We pinned the map to the wall and marked a blue spot in Innisfree Square, our first destination outside the lab.

As soon as we'd done that, we walked over to Innisfree Square with the GPS receiver and I tried to locate the place where I'd landed the day before. I was vaguely hoping to find the impressions left by the chair legs but either the grass had sprung back or I wasn't in exactly the right place. We recorded the position anyway and stored the coordinates in the receiver. Then we went back to the lab.

To calculate the distance we needed to take a GPS reading at my chair inside the cage. I couldn't get a good fix from there because the cage was shielding the receiver from the satellite transmissions, so I moved to one side of it and recorded the position there instead. I got out my laptop and we loaded the new navigation software. We'd soon worked out, between us, how to use it to calculate the straight-line distance between two sets of GPS coordinates at our latitude. Strictly speaking it was a geodesic line rather than a straight line, but over this sort of distance the error would be negligible.

Still on the laptop, I brought up our graph of distance against energy setting. It had a cluster of dots on it for each projection we'd made inside the lab. Now I could add the new data from Innisfree Square. The dot sat on its own, well up and to the right of the others. We looked at the pattern made by the dots.

"Looks to me like they could all lie on a straight line," Mike offered.

"We need longer projections to be certain. Also I need to project back to Innisfree Square to check that position. It's only approximate at the moment. We're getting there, Mike. We just have to put a bit more work in, that's all."

19

By now I was well settled into Mike's flat. Up to the time I'd moved in with him all our interaction had been in the college. Now, seeing the way he managed his personal life, I couldn't help but be impressed. I'm used to being ahead of everyone else academically, but I suppose I can be a bit unworldly when it comes to the basic skills of living. Mike is just the opposite; he's a master of survival. He's a more than passable cook and beyond that he's a fund of common sense on all sorts of matters. In fact he seems to be able to cope with every practical situation that life can throw at you— except one: strangely his street-wise instincts seem to desert him when it comes to dealing with women. In this respect, at least, I had the advantage, but then I've had a first class grounding in that department. It would be ungallant to go into too much detail. Let me just say that when I was sixteen my mother took me with her on a visit to some friends in France. I was a good-looking and precociously mature teenager, and I was quickly adopted by a circle of bored married women and divorcees who, unknown to my mother, took a close interest in my further education. That experience gave me a confidence with the opposite sex that has never left me, and in some way I think women sense it.

The moment I clapped eyes on Suzy I could see that poor old Mike was way out of his depth. She was a pretty little thing, all right, and I could see why he was so smitten. The trouble was, he just didn't know how to manage her. He wasn't so much shy as deferent, polite and anxious to please, whereas it was obvious to me that what she needed was a firm hand, excitement and a bit of action. I declined his offer of dinner that night, although I hadn't in fact eaten already, because I would have had to say how good it was and I didn't want to build him up further in Suzy's eyes. I thought it would be all right to accept a glass of wine. I was fairly offhand with Suzy on that first meeting, figuring that it would pique her interest, and obviously it did.

Over the next few weeks we started to go out as a threesome, usually to have dinner. I think the suggestion came from Suzy. I don't think Mike was all that keen, as he wanted her to himself, and that worked against him because he would end up on one side of the table looking sullen while Suzy and I would be on the other side, enjoying ourselves. And naturally there would be times when she or I would exchange some comment that he couldn't hear, and we would laugh and he would think we were having fun at his expense and give us a hard look. At the end of the evening Suzy always went home on her own and we went back to the flat. Nothing more would be said about it, although he was usually pretty quiet. I'm sure he felt uncomfortable about me and Suzy.

*

Apart from the minor complication of Suzy, things went on very much as before. Even if Mike had been a bit sulky the previous evening he'd be as enthusiastic as ever when he joined me in the lab the following afternoon. We kept adding to our toll of projections, gradually working further and further out. We always chose an open space, like a park or square, partly because it would be less dangerous but mainly because my sudden arrival would be less conspicuous. I did away with the chair for the same reason. We would identify the site on the map and then one or other of us would get on a bus and go to it with the GPS receiver and take a reading. Then back at the lab we'd calculate the energy we thought we needed, based on all the data we had up to that point, and I would allow myself to be projected there, carrying the GPS receiver with me. When I arrived I could check the coordinates and see how far out we were. Gradually the number of blue spots on the map of London increased, and with it the number of dots on the graph in my laptop. After doing this for three weeks or so it seemed a good time to take stock, so we sat down together with the laptop in front of us.

I pointed to the screen.

"The graph's a straight line out to about here."

"What is that in terms of distance?"

"About a mile. After that it curves over. That means you need more and more energy for each increase in distance."

"So what's the furthest we could go then, Rodge? I mean with the power we've got in the lab."

"I don't think we'd be seriously limited until we were out to about…" I pointed to the graph. "…here. Let's see where that is, geographically."

We went over to the map on the wall and I put a ruler against it.

"We could get out as far as the Blackwall Tunnel area," I said. "Beyond that, I think we'd be pushing it. Look, that's all right; this was only ever intended to be a prototype apparatus. I could do a whole lot more if I had an entire power station at my disposal."

We both laughed, but I wasn't joking entirely; I didn't see why the thing couldn't be scaled up in that way. I added:

"The important thing we've achieved, Mike, isn't the distance we can go, it's how precise we can be. We've got a lot of good data now. Within this radius of operation," I used a finger to draw a rough circle on the map, "we can predict quite accurately where I'm going to land."

"How accurately?"

"Well, if we always use the same GPS receiver to take the readings—"

"Which we always will."

"—which, as you say, we always will—we can be accurate to better than one metre."

Mike nodded. "That's impressive. So what do you want to do next?"

"Well, to start with what I'd like to do is extend the deadline for return. Two minutes isn't really long enough. Ten minutes would give me a bit more scope at the other end. But it's up to you, Mike. I do need you to be in the lab, and I appreciate that it's boring for you just waiting around for me."

"No, I can cope with that. The interesting part for me is what you get up to during the projections. As long as you give me a reasonably detailed account when you get back— you know, like you have been doing up to now—I don't mind waiting."

"I'll do that, of course. Look, would you like to swap places, have me project you for a change? Then you could experience it at first hand."

Mike shook his head straight away.

"No thanks, Rodge. Believe me, I have no ambitions

whatever in that direction."

It was the response I'd expected and secretly I was glad. I was still the only person in the world who knew what it felt like to travel in an instant to a place maybe two miles away and then exist in two places at once for the next few minutes.

*

From my point of view the ten-minute projections were a great success. It gave me a chance to get more skilled at handling my projected self independently from the one in the cage. Mike asked me to explain how I did it.

"Well, I'll try, Mike. You know the technique I developed for sorting out vision?"

"You concentrated on the new scene, didn't you, until you weren't aware of the cage any more."

"That's right. Well, this is very similar. First I focus my eyes on the new scene. When that's nice and solid I watch my limbs. As I move them, I pay close attention to the sensations. This gives me a feel for where they are and how they're moving in the new setting. Once I've done that I can stand up or walk or wave my arms around with my eyes closed if I want to."

"Well it obviously works. The only Rodge I can see is the one in the cage, but he barely moves. In fact while you're projected there's nothing happening at all. Maybe I could bring a radio in; at least it would help to pass the time."

"No—sorry, Mike, we can't do that."

"Why not?"

"Well, the one thing I haven't been able to do is separate out sound. Everything reaches me from both settings and I can't suppress any of it. I can cope with the hum of the equipment because it's a constant background, but anything more than that would be too confusing. No, I'm afraid things have got to stay totally quiet in the lab, otherwise I won't be able to make sense of what I hear when I've been projected. I'm sorry it's boring for you. Perhaps you could bring a book in, or do some of your coursework."

*

Things were running very smoothly now, and the procedure had become almost routine for both of us. Sometimes it took an effort of will to remind myself of the truly incredible thing we were doing. My mind was full of possibilities and experiments and I suppose I was even sifting through some of these in my sleep, because I woke up one morning with something new to try.

20

The question running through my mind was this: would it be possible to take some sort of receptacle with me and use it to bring an object back to the cage?

My first instinct was that it wouldn't work. I'd be able to carry a box with me; that wouldn't be a problem. But suppose I put a ball in the box at the other end? When Mike returned me to the cage, the box would surely pass through the ball or the ball through the box, and get left behind—in the same way as I passed through the wall of the cage and the wall of the building.

As I say, that was my initial reaction. But something about the symmetry of the situation made me try the calculation. I started by considering a spherical container, a resonating shell surrounding a non-resonating object. It turned out that the forces on one side balanced out those on the other, so the object always stayed inside. After that it was only half an hour's work to generalize the calculation from a sphere to any irregularly shaped container. I concluded that it should work, and the only proviso was that the container had to be completely closed.

"What do you think, Mike?" I asked after I'd explained the idea to him.

"Well to be honest I couldn't follow the calculation, but I think we ought to give it a try. What have we got to lose? Why don't you buy a bag or something tomorrow morning, while I'm in my class? Then we can have a shot in the afternoon."

The following morning I went down to High Street Kensington and bought a leather duffel bag. A nylon one would have been lighter, but I liked the design of the leather one better. It had a kind of flap inside that went over the contents and a good tight draw-string closure. When Mike came to the lab that afternoon we discussed the whole thing in more detail while the equipment was warming up. We decided to make the projection to St James's Park. I'd been there before. At the Buckingham Palace end there were some nice flower gardens, and one of them had a rockery. The plan was to bring back one of the rocks.

*

I arrived not far from the path that ran along the side of the lake, carrying my new duffel bag. I looked around me but the only people I could see were a good distance away. The Palace was just visible over the tops of the trees. The royal standard was flying; Her Majesty must be in residence. I had the fleeting thought that it might be fun to project myself inside there some time. Present myself to the monarch. That would be a chuckle—marvellous publicity too! Still, one thing at a time. I had my bearings now so I started to walk briskly down towards the gardens. The rockery was just where I'd remembered seeing it.

I took another quick look around but there was no one close by. I stepped briskly forward and took hold of a rock. I couldn't shift it. I stepped back and looked at it in disbelief. It wasn't that big, how could it be that heavy? For a moment I thought it had been cemented in. Then it dawned on me. Because my mass was being shared between the two places, my muscles were only half their normal weight, and that meant they were only half as strong. I hadn't noticed it before because all they'd been moving was my limbs, and their weight had halved too, so everything was in proportion. I thought about it for a bit. Then I opened the bag and put it on the ground. I chose a rock that wasn't too big, imagined it to be twice the size it was, and put in the right amount of effort. It came up without much difficulty and I dropped it into the bag. Then I closed the flap over the top of the bag, drew the closure tight, and gave Mike the signal.

As soon as Mike had returned me to the cage he came round and opened the door. We looked expectantly at each other. Then I undid the draw-string and we looked in the bag.

"It's still there. Mike, it worked!"

Mike punched the air and shouted, "Yes!"

Even though my calculations had predicted it would happen I could hardly believe it. We took the bag into the lab, put it on the bench and Mike lifted out the rock. He grinned and handed it to me. As I took it from him I almost threw it up in the air.

"Watch out, Rodge! What are you doing?"

I laughed. "Nothing. I was expecting it to be twice as heavy, that's all!"

Of course it felt light because I was back to normal strength now. I explained that part to Mike. Then we left the rock on the bench and went back to his flat. I was in a great mood the whole evening. My head was so full of possibilities I could hardly sleep at all that night.

I got up earlier than was usual for me and joined Mike for breakfast. He liked to have toast and marmalade and tea for breakfast; I only ever had coffee. I brought my mug to the table and sat down with him.

I took a gulp of coffee.

"I've been thinking, Mike. We're ready to go public with this now. We could do a demonstration for the Royal Society! We could publish it in Nature! I bet we'd make the front cover! You can be a co-author, Mike."

"No, thanks."

I put down my coffee mug in surprise.

"Why? We'll be famous!"

"Infamous more like."

I couldn't understand it. He was usually quite enthusiastic about what we were doing. Perhaps he hadn't woken up fully. I decided to try again.

"But Mike! Think of what you could do! You could get oxygen, food and water to people trapped in a tunnel or a mine collapse. You could be at a business meeting miles away in an instant! I don't know what the ultimate range would be. Matter waves aren't refracted or reflected like electromagnetic waves so the curvature of the earth might be a problem. But even so the potential applications are endless…"

Mike stopped me dead in my tracks.

"You're so brilliant, Rodge, and yet you so haven't got it."

21

"Why, what do you mean I haven't got it?"

"I mean you're going to have to keep a lid on this—you know that, don't you? It's far too dangerous. Right now you're the only person who can do it. Okay, but once people know it can be done you won't be able to stop it spreading. Look at nuclear weapons. At one time only the superpowers could make them. Now any tin-pot bloody country can do it."

I suppose I was still looking blank. He regarded me patiently.

"Look, Rodge, you can pass through walls, right? Do you have any idea how disastrous it would be if this technology got out? It would be the worst thing to hit civilized society. It would be like locks were never invented. You can go anywhere—and so can anyone else if they get hold of it. Thieves will go in and clean out banks and post offices. Paedophiles will enter nurseries. Single women will be raped in their own bedrooms and no one will ever know who it was or how they got in. Do I need to go on?"

I realized that, of course; I just hadn't thought it through in quite those terms. I felt quite unsettled. When you were dealing with the physics you knew where you were. Now Mike was talking about the implications for society and that was less familiar territory. I'd never seen any of that as a serious barrier to announcing the discovery. What had I been working for all this time? So that my work could go unreported, unexploited, unacclaimed? I couldn't let go.

"Well, what about the armed services, and MI5, and MI6?" I challenged. "They'd keep it quiet. And they'd be interested all right. They could enter foreign embassies and terrorist headquarters and steal secret plans, all that spy stuff. Think what James Bond could do with it! You wouldn't even need a James Bond—any filing clerk could do it! And if you had multiple set-ups like this one you could transport a whole division of crack commandos behind enemy lines!"

Mike's voice was almost weary. "Look, Rodge, if the secret service took it on it would be for one of two reasons: to develop it or to suppress it. Either way there's a good chance they'd quietly arrange for you to meet with a fatal accident, just to be certain the secret never got to the other side. If you flogged it to a foreign power it would be the same, only they'd probably kill you quicker, while the Brits were still fooling around with the paperwork."

I sagged in my seat. I had the heavy feeling that he was right.

"All right, Mike. I take your point, but if I can't publicize it and I can't sell it, what can I do with it? It's too good a thing just to let it go."

He crunched into another piece of toast and marmalade and regarded me thoughtfully. Finally he said, in a quiet way:

"It seems to me that the strength of your position is precisely that no one else does know. If you keep it that way you have options. You stay a totally free agent."

Before I could ask him exactly what he meant he'd jumped up and grabbed his jacket and a slim document case off a chair.

"Got to go," he said, "I'll come by at three o'clock."

"Oh. Yes, all right. See you later."

And I was left to my thoughts.

*

Usually I had the equipment up and running by the time Mike arrived in the lab, so that we could get straight on with the experiments. Only this time I didn't. He saw at a glance that nothing was switched on. He didn't seem in the least surprised by that. Nor was he surprised when I said I wanted to have a talk about the future direction of the work. I suggested we went back to his flat. We didn't say any more about it until we'd got there. He made some tea and we sat down at the kitchen table.

"Look, Mike, I've been thinking. I have a problem, and I have a solution."

"Okay, I'm listening."

"We've talked about this before. I have a large overdraft at the bank, and the manager is calling it in. He's not bluffing; he's the sort of vindictive bastard who'll make a personal crusade of it. Any time now he's going to be sending in the heavies to collect payment or goods to an equivalent value. They don't know I've moved to your place, but they'll track me down soon enough, you can be sure of that. So I'm afraid this involves you too, because it's your door they'll be hammering on. I shouldn't think the bailiffs will be too particular about whether they're removing your stuff or mine. They could take our laptops, furniture, carpets, curtains, kitchen stuff, everything. We'll end up sitting on the floor. I'm sorry. I shouldn't have got you into this in the first place."

"You don't have to be sorry. I knew all that when I took you in."

"Well, don't think I don't appreciate it, Mike. But I'm not going to sit here and wait for it to happen. For a long time now I've been racking my brains for a way out of this. It seems to me that if I paid off a reasonable sum on account, as a show of good intent—you know, something like five thousand pounds—I could probably avoid the unpleasantness and buy myself some time. But where do I get five thousand pounds? That's the problem. With me so far?"

"All the way."

"All right. Well, the solution has been staring me in the face, only I didn't see it until now. Look Mike, I can gain access to virtually anywhere in Central London. I don't need a key, I can get in without anybody seeing me come or go, and no one except the two of us knows I can do it. It's even better than that: I can take a bag with me and bring stuff back."

"What are you saying?"

"Well, if it's all right with you, I thought I'd rob a few banks."

22

I'd been deliberately blunt to see what kind of reaction it would evoke. Frankly I was expecting an immediate outburst of righteous indignation about the immorality of the suggestion, my lack of principle, and so on. Instead he simply waited patiently for me to go on. It was as if he knew it was coming all along. It even crossed my mind that he had, in some way, planted the idea in my head, but I dismissed the thought. Mike was far too uncomplicated for that.

"All right," I continued. "You'll notice that I said banks, plural. I'm not thinking of large strong rooms and vaults. People spend months and months planning heists like that. They need a big team, and if they're going to have enough to share around they have to lift really large amounts of money. For me it's much easier. I can be in and out—I could do three in a morning without any problem. So I can afford to take less each time. I'm talking about cleaning out what's behind the counters. I don't know how much they keep there but it must be worth a few thousand on every trip. It'll soon mount up."

Still Mike was saying nothing, just watching me carefully.

"So I'd like you to help me do it, in two ways. Obviously by manning the equipment in the usual way. But secondly by helping me to establish the coordinates for the projection sites. We'd share the targets between us. All you have to do is go to the counter, take a reading with the GPS receiver, and store it. Obviously you have to be discreet about it but the GPS does look a bit like a mobile phone, so that shouldn't be too difficult. The rest is straightforward. What do you say?"

Mike was thoughtful. Again I was expecting a deluge of moral objections but all he said was:

"And what's in it for me?"

I was taken aback. I hadn't thought it through that far.

"Obviously we'd split the proceeds, fifty-fifty," I stammered out quickly. "I'm taking the major risks, but I can't do it without you."

There was another pause.

"Okay. But first I think we need to refine your plans somewhat."

I was so relieved that he was going along with the idea that I didn't care.

"Anything you say."

"Well, for a start I think you should cut your teeth on a softer target. I would suggest smaller post offices, with one or at the most two, positions. Hit them at a quiet time, maybe around ten to nine in the morning, just before they're open to the public—less chance of being seen. Choose a good morning, like the day they stock up for paying out state pensions—I think it's Thursday. That way there'll be more money in the drawers."

Was he really responding spontaneously, I wondered? It seemed like he'd been thinking about this for weeks. He went on:

"You'll need to do several of them in quick succession. Once word gets around they may start installing counter-measures. The police may put more people on standby so they can mount a quicker response to alarms; there could be extra police patrols, maybe even security guards. You need to do a number of hits in three or four days at most. That means you can't do all of them before nine in the morning. And that in turn means you'll have to do some when not just counter clerks are around but members of the public could be as well. So you'll need to disguise yourself."

"What, you mean stocking over the face, or black balaclava with two eye-holes?" I asked.

He smiled wryly. "Something like that. The balaclava is good: no mouth, no hair colour or hair line visible. Only I'm not sure if I know a handy terrorist outfitters in this part of London."

We chuckled.

"What do you suggest then?"

"You know the expedition place where I got the GPS? They have everything. People who go to the South Pole or up high mountains wear a form of balaclava—covers the head and mouth, just leaves a gap for the eyes. Usually in high visibility colours rather than black but that's okay. It'll work fine. We can always dye it black if we want to."

"All right. What else?"

"Well, the counter clerk could be male or female, and either way they're not going to take kindly to a polite request to empty the till into your bag. They've probably been told not to resist a robbery but they could send the alarm to the police without you seeing the move. And the top drawer doesn't contain all that much money. If you want a better haul you're going to need something to persuade them to unlock the bottom drawer."

I hadn't even realized there was a bottom drawer. Persuade them? What was he talking about?

"Do you mean a gun?"

"Yep, a handgun would be fine. The trouble is, this is

England. You can't just go into a shop and buy one over the counter. In fact you can't buy one at all."

"Criminals get them."

"Yeah, but we don't have those kind of connections. It doesn't matter. You don't need a real gun: you're not going to shoot anyone, you're only going to threaten them. You just need something that looks like a real gun."

"There are plastic kits. I could make one."

"Wouldn't have the weight. No, we can do better than that. I think at least one company makes air pistols that are replicas of the real thing. They use CO_2 capsules. Hang on a bit. I'll look them up on the Internet. You can clear up the tea things while I'm doing it."

Mike normally kept his laptop on the end of a counter in the kitchen, connected to the mains and broadband. That way it was always charged and ready for use. He booted it up and ten minutes later he beckoned me over. The last web page was still on the screen.

"I was right," he said. "See, if you were going for a real gun I'd say you needed an automatic—Colt, Browning, Walther, something like that. But for a gun that really looks like a gun I don't think you can beat a revolver. Like this one." He pointed to the screen. "It's a replica Smith and Wesson. We can get one with a six-inch barrel. Looks the business, eh? But it's actually an air pistol."

It certainly looked convincing.

"How are we going to get one?"

"Easy. This site lists the stockists. There's one in Knightsbridge. I'll get one for you tomorrow. All you have to do is get used to cocking it and handling it as if it was the real thing."

"How much is it going to cost?"

Mike shrugged.

"Doesn't matter, does it? We'll get that back and more in the first job."

I nodded. "Of course. Okay. Sounds good. What else?"

"Coordinates. I understand what you're saying. You want to take a reading right at the counter and then add a bit so that you land on the other side. That's okay. We can do that with the GPS."

"How?"

"Just a minute."

He went into the kitchen and I heard a drawer opening. He came back with a steel tape measure and stretched it across the kitchen counter top. "Allow a bit for the wall and partition..." he stripped some more tape out "...bit more for the chair... two metres should do it." He let the tape retract. "We'll set up your destination as a way point. All you do is add the two metres and direction to the reading you've got and it will give you the coordinates you want."

"That's good. I hadn't realized we could do that."

"Yeah, the guy showed me in the shop. Seems like that built-in compass is going to be useful after all; you can take a bearing at the same time as you're recording the coordinates. Mmm, I just had another thought!"

"What's that?"

"Well if we've got the compass bearing we can work out which way you should be facing in the cage when I project you. Then you'll land pointing in exactly the right direction."

"Oh, nice touch, Mike! Otherwise it would take me a few moments to get orientated. One thing, though. When I'm taking all these readings, is there some way I could avoid having to go right up to the counter? I know I'll be wearing a balaclava when I'm doing the actual job but I'm still a bit worried they might recognize me or my voice."

"It's very unlikely. They're dealing with hundreds of people every day. And you won't be measuring all the locations; we'll be sharing them out between us."

"I didn't say it was rational, Mike. It's just that I don't feel all that comfortable about it."

"Well I'll tell you what. While I'm out I'll find a good hardware store and buy an ultrasonic tape measure. Contractors and surveyors and estate agents use them for measuring up rooms. It's only a small plastic box with a button and an LCD readout. If you just stand there with it people will think you're texting or something. You don't even have to join a queue. You can stand back as far as you like and bounce the beam off the counter or the glass. Use it to get the exact distance from where you're standing to the counter; we'll add two metres afterwards to get to the point on the other side. Then you quietly swap it for the GPS receiver and you take the coordinates and compass bearing. Put it up to your ear and walk out of the place talking. Nobody will turn a hair."

"That's a good idea. Are they expensive, these ultrasonic gadgets?"

"No. Thirty or forty quid. Don't worry. We'll get that back too."

We sat talking and planning for another hour and a half, breaking the project down into subtasks, assigning responsibilities and drawing up a schedule. It was amazing how easy it was to switch from planning an experiment to planning a crime. I found it gave me the same buzz, the same sense of excitement and anticipation, as embarking on a new piece of research. The skills, too, transferred readily from one sphere to the other. In both cases it was a matter of preparing and organizing, of predicting all the possible outcomes and modifying the design to take account of them. We got as far as we could and then called it a day. I would start work on it in the morning and Mike would make that important trip to the shops after his class in the afternoon.

*

The business of setting up the robberies was uppermost in my mind, of course, but whenever I stopped thinking about that I'd get depressed all over again. My research project had been a huge intellectual and technical challenge. For more than two years I'd done virtually nothing else, and working on it had got me deep into debt. The one thing that had kept me going was the prospect of showing all those blinkered idiots out there that there was another way of looking at matter, and proving it with a technology that would transform people's lives and make me a household name. And now that I'd finally succeeded—succeeded beyond my wildest dreams—where were the rewards? Mike had opened my eyes all right. The world wasn't ready for my discovery; society wasn't mature enough to handle it in a civilized way. I couldn't even publish my findings. It was enough to make anyone feel bitter.

Well, all right. I would commit myself totally to the new activity. If I couldn't profit from my research scientifically, I would make damned sure I'd enjoy the benefit of it in every possible way.

And I do mean every possible way.

23

We hit the first post office the following Tuesday, at a quarter to nine in the morning. There was a skinny, elderly woman behind the counter and I materialized right behind her. I was in luck; she was just transferring money from the bottom drawer to the top drawer. I put a hand quickly over her mouth and pulled her back from the counter to keep her away from alarm buttons and kick plates. It gave her the hell of a fright. I gestured with the gun that I wanted the drawers emptied into my duffel bag. She didn't need any persuasion but her hands were shaking so much I thought she was going to empty the money all over the floor. Somehow she managed to get the contents of both drawers into the bag.

"Lie down," I said to her.

That seemed hard for her. She got as far as her hands and knees. I decided that was good enough.

I took a couple of steps back, transferred my awareness to the cage and lifted my arm, the signal for Mike to quench the resonance. And then I was back. It was as simple as that.

Mike helped me transfer about four thousand pounds in used notes from the duffel bag into a sports bag he'd brought along for the purpose. It wasn't a huge amount but we were only just beginning.

I said, "Okay, what's next on the list?"

Mike and I had spent the last few days visiting post offices. We had the coordinates for more than twenty suitable targets now and we'd drawn up a schedule. We would simply work down the list.

"Target Number Two is Shepherds Bush," Mike said. He was already putting in the settings.

The clerk had just brought in the till for the day's transactions. She didn't see me land behind her. I sized her up. She was slightly overweight, dyed blonde, looked to be in her late thirties. Could be the owner or the wife of the owner. I went through the same moves as before, putting a hand over her mouth, pulling her away from the counter, and then pointing the gun at the drawers and at my duffel bag. She emptied the top drawer into the bag and then hesitated. I pointed the gun at the bottom drawer and then held it to her head. She fumbled out a key and turned it in the lock. It didn't open. I started to get agitated. She was making an attempt to say something so I let the pressure off her mouth a little.

"There's a time delay on the lock," she gasped.

"'ow long?"

"About two minutes."

I hadn't anticipated that. I was tempted to call it a day. Then I thought, *stay cool, it doesn't make any difference.* I was pretty sure she hadn't been able to raise the alarm so there was still time. We were in line with the door, but it had posters on it, so we couldn't easily be seen from the street. The street door was still locked, of course, and it would stay that way if she wasn't there to open it. Even if someone else came in I'd still be able to disappear with what I had.

"Well, we'll just have to wait then, won't we?" I said keeping my voice very rough.

There was a chair at the back of the counter area. I reached out and hooked it with one foot, brought it closer, and dropped her into it.

"Put your hands on your head and keep 'em there," I said. I was standing behind the chair and keeping the gun where she could see it. She was breathing very rapidly, her chest rising and falling. I reached my free left hand into her blouse, slipped it under her bra, and gave her right breast a good palping, just while we were waiting. She was starting to shake all over. I was thinking about dipping my hand under the waistband of her skirt when I heard a click from the lock. I let go of her and motioned with the gun for her to empty the contents into my bag.

I watched her dropping the money into the bag.

"All of it," I snarled.

She licked her lips and said huskily, "That's all of it."

I snatched the bag from her, closed the flap over the money, and drew the string tight.

"Face down on the floor," I commanded.

She did as she was told. I put a foot on one plump buttock and she shivered. It gave me some more ideas but there wasn't time.

"Don't look round."

I signalled Mike and I was back in the lab emptying the bag for the second time.

I was starting to enjoy myself.

Target Number Three was in Notting Hill. By the time I arrived it was nearly nine o'clock. It looked as if they were running late because there was no one on the counter, although the door to the counter area was ajar. I peeked around it, just in time to see a man walking unhurriedly away down a short corridor. I followed him to a room at the back. He was grey-haired, probably in his fifties, but he had a wiry build. He'd just opened a safe, which was built into the wall at about head height, and he was withdrawing a box. I stepped up behind him, put a hand over his mouth, and jabbed the gun into his cheek so that he could see and feel what it was. I had decided that it would be fun if the accounts the police got from these different raids varied, so I put on a rough south London accent. It wasn't that good, but with everything else that was going on I thought he might overlook that.

"Don' make a sound and do wha' I tell ya," I barked, "unless you'd like to see yer brains decoratin' that wall. Know wha' I mean? Just nod yer 'ead if ya do."

He'd gone rigid with the shock and surprise. I jabbed again with the barrel of the gun and he nodded his head rapidly.

Looking over his shoulder I could see that the inside of the safe was divided into two. On the left hand side were three compartments, arranged one above the other, each occupied by a lockable box. He'd been withdrawing the topmost box. I recognized it as a till, basically the bottom drawer that I'd emptied on the previous two raids. The right hand side of the safe was undivided; there were a few documents and boxes towards the back, but no money so far as I could see.

"Take art that till and open it up," I said.

He withdrew the box and placed it in the right-hand section of the safe. He reached into his pocket, presumably for the key, but I wasn't taking chances and I reacted quickly, pressing the gun harder against his cheek.

"Nice an' easy, now," I said.

His hand came out slowly with a bunch of keys on the end of a long chain. He fitted a key into the lock and turned it. My duffel bag was still hoisted over my left shoulder. I shrugged it down to my left hand and passed it in front of him.

"Now open this bag up and frow the money in," I said, gesturing with the gun in my right hand. It seemed this was the opportunity he was looking for. He grabbed my right wrist with his left hand, jerking it forward and at the same time stabbing his right elbow back into my ribs. It caught me by surprise and it hurt, but I managed to keep hold of the gun. Then he tried to pull me over his extended right leg in a judo throw. Unfortunately for him he was standing close to the safe and he didn't have enough room. I slammed my cupped left hand into the back of his head, driving it forward into the frame of the safe. He gave a shout of pain and I felt him go a bit slack. I was mad as hell, so I did it again, even harder, and his knees started to buckle. I didn't let him drop, though. I plunged my left hand into the back of his shirt collar and twisted it as I held him up. He was spluttering.

"D'ye really want t'be a dead 'ero?" I asked him grimly. "If y'do, then just try somep'n stoopid like that again."

I was quite pleased at being able to keep the accent up. I added slowly, with special menace:

"Now do wha' I told yer and stop fuckin' about."

I eased the pressure on the collar and he put a hand to his throat, still gasping. I prodded him with the gun and he quickly wiped his eyes, shook his head, and reached for the box. When he'd emptied the money into the duffel bag I said:

"Now do the same wiv the next till."

"I haven't got the key," he said.

His voice was shaky but still defiant. There was no way he hadn't got the key. I was pretty sure he was the owner, but even if he wasn't he would know where spare keys were kept.

I put the barrel firmly under his chin.

"Don' fuck with me, mate, I swear I'll blow your fuckin' 'ead off."

"All right, all right."

He fumbled with the keys on that long chain and opened the next box. When he'd emptied that one I got him to empty the third.

"Now get on the floor," I commanded.

He got onto his hands and knees, too slowly. I kicked him as hard as I could in the ribs, and he howled with pain. I was murderously angry with this little man who had the temerity to interfere with my plans. I stamped on the seat of his pants to push him to the floor.

"Go on, flat on the floor. Arms above yer 'ead. Spread yer legs," I shouted at him, while I pulled the drawstring tight on the duffel bag. Spreading his legs was just a little finesse on my part. It enabled me to put a good kick between them, leaving him writhing in agony, as I gave Mike the signal to kill the resonance.

Things swam and I was back in the cage. I was still breathing hard but my improvisation had paid off handsomely. The haul was a lot better than a counter raid alone. Mike wanted to set the coordinates for another target but he didn't know what had just happened and I gestured to him to call a halt. The adrenaline was still flowing and I wasn't ready to start again. I left him sorting out the money and went over to the bench to make some coffee.

That little sod was probably ex-army or something. He was insured for the money so why did he have to have a go at me? Thinking about it, what I found interesting was my own reaction. When we'd started this caper it wouldn't have entered into my head that I would actually want to shoot anyone. Yet if that chap had tried his luck again I have no doubt whatever that I'd have used the gun on him, I was that mad. I'd even forgotten for the moment that the gun wasn't real.

24

We hit another post office later the same morning and three more in the afternoon. On each trip I cleared the counters. All these post offices were grouped in one area, to make it look as if thieves had travelled from one to another in quick succession. That way post offices in other parts of London would think it was planned and executed by a local gang, and they wouldn't be expecting to be hit themselves. It was Mike's idea.

We did seven more post offices the following day. By that time the Press had got hold of it. The *Evening Standard* carried an item on our first three raids. I was tweaking the equipment at the time, so Mike read it out to me.

"It says here: 'It appears that the armed robber laid in wait for the postmistress, Mrs. Lucille Ambrose, and attacked her when she came to the counter in the morning. He subjected her to a violent sexual assault and got away with a small amount of cash...' Sexual assault?"

"She's just milking it, Mike. She's probably going to claim compensation so she's laying it on thick. Go on."

Mike gave me a searching look, then returned to the newspaper.

"'Following the incident Mrs. Ambrose was taken to Charing Cross Hospital and is being held there under observation.' You weren't that rough with her, were you, Rodge?"

"Of course not. What else does it say?"

"'In spite of her terrifying ordeal, brave Mrs. Ambrose agreed to help the police with their enquiries. A police spokeswoman said that a description of the assailant will be issued in due course.'"

"I don't know what kind of description she could give them. She could see my hands so she knows I'm white and she can say roughly how tall I am. That's about it. Anything about the other jobs?"

"There's a bit here about the third one. 'During his army career Mr. Barton served with distinction in a number of postings, including Northern Ireland and The Falklands. He attempted to resist the robber, but he was overpowered and subjected to a vicious beating. He is currently recovering in hospital.' Rodge…?"

"He had a go at me, Mike. I didn't have any choice. Anyway it wasn't as bad as all that—they always exaggerate, these reporters. Is that it?"

"Just a statement from the police to warn members of the public. It says 'The robber is dangerous and in no circumstances should he be approached or tackled.'"

"Nothing about how the thief gained access?"

"Nope, that's it. Obviously the cops haven't a clue so they're not saying anything."

*

On the Thursday we did another seven post offices, starting a little earlier to take advantage of the pension payouts. Mike was neglecting his course, but he seemed reconciled to that. We put the money into a suitcase, all ninety-five thousand pounds of it. It seemed like a good week's work to me.

*

We weren't planning any more raids, at least not for the moment. Mike wasn't coming in to the lab; he was catching up on his studies. The sudden inactivity left me filled with a restless energy. I couldn't settle down to anything. The events of the last week had given me a feeling of exhilaration, and it wasn't just the money: it was the feeling of potency. I could go anywhere, do anything. I'd barely scratched the surface of what was possible. It's true there were limits. I couldn't do a whole lot about money that was locked in safes. Usually a room with a safe would be kept locked, and unless I knew exactly where it was I wouldn't be able to set coordinates for it, much less open the actual safe. I'd just been lucky to find the ex-army chap opening his, and even that could have ended badly if he'd taken a better shot at me. Daytime raids on jewellery stores or places like that would be risky too, and then I'd have the problem of fencing the stuff. I had no idea how to develop the contacts, and I didn't want to do that anyway; involving other people was a sure route to disaster. But there were plenty of other possibilities.

I took the Tube to Piccadilly Circus and walked endlessly around Soho. Late on Saturday evening it was still warm and some of the clubs were spilling out onto the pavements. Noisy, mindless kids, drinking wine and beer. Teenage girls with long blonde hair, dresses cut low to show off their cleavages. Girls in short tight skirts, or longer skirts slit to reveal pale, well-turned thighs. They didn't know what it was all about. I could show them.

I found myself wondering about my appetite for women. It wasn't the first time I'd thought about it. Was it just a normal masculine drive or was it something I'd inherited from my father? It was curious to think that something like that might have been passed down to me. If it had, I didn't mind. I didn't hate my father. To hate someone you need to have had some sort of adverse relationship, and I'd had no relationship with him at all; it was more like I'd never had a father. I knew he'd pretty much ruined my mother's life, and I suppose I should have resented him for her sake, but then I wasn't close enough to her for it to matter. It was family history to me, as I might have read it in a dry book. It didn't stir up any emotions, one way or the other.

Another girl emerged onto the pavement, a slim girl in tightly haunched jeans, with two or three inches of bare midriff showing. I watched her, savouring the sense of power. It would be so easy. I'd just follow her home, watch the light come on in her bedroom. Set the GPS coordinates in the street, take an ultrasonic distance reading, go back to the lab and project straight into her room. I fantasized about gagging her, tying her to the bed…

I watched her as she walked up the street with her friends. It was no good. I'd risk attracting attention by going into the Department in the early hours. In any case it wouldn't take Mike long to twig what I was up to. He'd never stand for it; he was too straight-laced for that. No, I needed to make another set-up somewhere else. My equipment had been cobbled together from what was available. It was the sort of string-and-sealing-wax prototype you had to start with in research. But now I knew exactly what was required and I could do it all so much more elegantly.

Wherever I set it up, I'd need a good power source. I'd have to buy a disused factory, one where they'd run a lot of three-phase electrical machines or a big induction furnace. It would take a lot of money. That was the major problem; the rest wasn't difficult. The lasers were commercially available, and I didn't need the extra adjustments any more. The drives to the photodiodes and the microwave generators were pretty standard. I could over-specify everything to make it really stable and reliable. If I linked all the power supplies and the charging circuits I should be able to initiate the whole procedure automatically. Then I could use a remote control from the cage to project myself and bring myself back. I wouldn't be tied to the college, so I could come and go as I pleased. I'd dispense with Mike, of course; I wouldn't need him any more. Then I could do anything I liked.

*

The post office robberies were news, of course, but people have short memories for such things. It only takes a gruesome murder, or a terrorist attack, or a win for England at cricket, to put it out of their minds. After a few days I phoned my bank and made an appointment to see the Manager the following Wednesday. By that time, I thought, I could do it without raising suspicions about my sudden affluence.

I got to the bank about fifteen minutes early. Only two of the three counter positions were manned; there was a chap and a girl, and I didn't recognize either of them. That was good; I didn't particularly want to be seen there by Suzy. I went to the enquiries desk.

"Can I help you?"

She was Indian, I think. Her complexion was dark, and her hair and eyes were even darker. I thought she could have been quite beautiful in an exotic sort of way, until she smiled and I saw the two long front teeth with a gap between them. Her badge said "Nadine". I held up a large envelope for her to see, and said quietly:

"I have a sizeable deposit to make. Do you think we could use a private room?"

"Certainly. What's the name, please?"

"Dukas."

"Just one moment."

She picked up the phone and punched a number.

"Caroline? Can you see a customer? Mr. Dukas. He's at the enquiries desk."

She put the phone down, turned to me, and smiled toothily.

"Caroline will be with you shortly."

A few moments later a tall red-head appeared at the desk and said, "Would you like to come through?"

I followed her down a short corridor, watching her white and green flowered dress move over gaunt hips. Not bad, but a bit willowy for my taste.

She led the way to a small room, empty except for a couple of chairs and a table with a computer monitor on it. She motioned me to a chair and took the other chair herself, sweeping her skirt under her thighs with one hand as she sat down.

"Now, how can I help you?"

"I'd like to deposit this in my account," I said, sliding the envelope over to her. I took my bank card out of my wallet and put that on the desk as well.

The envelope contained five thousand pounds in twenty-pound notes. She took a peek at it and then excused herself for a moment. When she came back she had a deposit slip and a portable machine for counting bank notes. She made pretty short work of it. Then she filled in the deposit slip for me, taking the account number from my bank card. She tore off the receipt portion and handed it to me.

"That's fine," she said brightly. "Is there anything else I can do for you?"

"I have an appointment with the manager at two forty-five."

"If you'd like to wait here I'll just see if he's free."

I'd made up my mind to swallow my pride and play the repentant sinner. Even so, the mere sight of the man made my gorge rise again.

"Do have a seat Mister Dukas—oh, excuse me, *Doctor* Dukas." He gave his steely, condescending smile. "Now what can we do for you?"

"You know, Mr. Meredrew, our conversation a couple of weeks ago came as something of a shock to me. I'd been totally immersed in my research, and I hadn't realized how out-of-hand things had got."

He said nothing, just watched me closely. On someone else the slightly upturned lips and crinkling of the eyes would have registered as a smile, but not on this cold fish.

"I just wanted you to know that I've been taking steps to, er, correct the situation. I've rearranged my personal affairs and a moment ago I deposited five thousand pounds in my account. It's only a start, I know, but I plan to be making regular deposits over the next few months. I should be in the black again within about six months."

"Well now, that is most welcome news. I'm delighted to hear it. Of course," he leaned forward and smiled even more ingratiatingly, "we'll continue to monitor the progress of your account so that we can let you know in good time if there seems to be any further problem."

"Thank you," I said, through gritted teeth.

"Is there anything else we can help you with at this time?"

"No, I just… no, that's all."

He got up and extended a clammy hand, which I released as soon as possible. "Thank you *so* much for coming in, Mister, er Doctor, Dukas. I'll see you out."

As soon as I was outside I wiped my hand on my trousers and breathed deeply to rid my lungs of the air I'd been obliged to share with that loathsome creature. It had been hard, it had been humiliating, but it was done: for the moment he was off my back. I swore that some day, somehow, I would make him pay for this episode. My favoured option involved a red-hot poker.

25

Her clothes came off on our first date. When I say "date" I mean the first time Suzy and I were able to get together without the watchful Mike in tow. Her girlfriend had gone away for a few days so we used her flat. I've had better sex, but only with very experienced women. One of the French ladies, in particular, sticks in my mind. She taught me a lot. She told me she used to be a dancer. I could just imagine the sort of dancing she did.

Suzy put up a token protest but I knew how to deal with it. I'm pretty sure all the lights went on for her, and there weren't any protests after that. We used her flat for the next two days, but then her girlfriend came back. After that it was just a question of where to go. She borrowed her girlfriend's little Renault once and we went out into the country and did it under the stars. The ground was lumpy so I let her sit on me. Then I turned her around; I preferred it like that because I could feel the squash of her cool buttocks in my loins. She said it hurt her a bit but I noticed she didn't stop. At the end she was still trembling. Quite a little number, Suzy, when you lit her fire.

It wasn't all sex. She tried to find out a bit more about me, and she wanted to know about the research I was doing. So I showed her one of my notebooks and started to work through a calculation—actually it was the calculation I'd used to establish that I could bring objects back to the cage.

It had a lot of triple integrals and vector algebra in it. As I'd anticipated, she glazed over in half a minute. She didn't ask me again, which was the way I wanted it. It didn't seem to bother her. Mostly it was the physical thing that kept us together. So far as I was concerned it was the only thing.

Towards the end of May, Mike sat his M.Sc. exams. On some pretext I had a look at his timetable. His last paper was a multiple choice and it was in the afternoon, so Suzy took some time off and came over to the flat. That was how he found out. He must have finished the examination early and decided to call it a day. When we heard the key in the front door we looked at each other for one shocked moment and then leapt out of bed. I just had time to pull on a pair of trousers. Suzy grabbed my dressing gown and slipped it on. He must have heard something in the lounge because he opened the door and came straight in without a care in the world. I was standing there, naked to the waist, Suzy was wiping her tousled hair back from her eyes, and the convertible sofa was a rumpled bed. He took it all in at a glance. I was stuck for words, but Suzy surprised me. She walked up to Mike, gathered him by the arm and asked him how the exam went. I noticed him glance down and away from her front where the dressing gown was gaping slightly and his mouth set a little.

"I thought you liked me," he said gruffly.

Actually I think he meant to put some emphasis on "me" but he couldn't quite bring himself to do it.

"But I do like you, Mike," she said soothingly. "I like you very much. Now please don't look so glum. We're all going to be good friends."

Still holding on to his arm she led him towards the kitchen, glancing over her shoulder at me and shooting her eyes meaningfully around the room. I got the message: I had to clean up fast.

I converted the bed back into a sofa, stowed the sheets and blankets in a drawer, gathered up Suzy's scattered clothes, put them on a chair and laid her skirt on the top of the pile to hide her underwear, straightened out the other chairs and looked round the room. As an afterthought I pulled the chair with Suzy's clothes over to the corner so that it was less obvious. By the time I went into the kitchen I'd recovered my equilibrium. Suzy had made a mug of tea for herself and Mike and the two of them were sitting at the table. She was still in my dressing-gown, of course, but she showed no signs of being in a hurry to get dressed. Mike was sitting forward with both arms on the table, and Suzy's posture echoed his, except that her hand was resting on one of Mike's.

I stood there, feeling a bit clumsy.

"You see how it is, don't you, Mike?" I said. "It couldn't be helped. Sometimes it's just a matter of chemistry."

Suzy's eyes stopped me from saying anything more.

"I've been over all that with him," she said, "and he's been perfectly sweet about it."

"Good old Mike," I said, and sat down at the table myself. There was a bit of a silence, and then I added, "Look, now this is all out in the open would it be all right if Suzy moved into the flat with us? We have the room, and it would be a lot more fun with the three of us."

Suzy shot me a sharp look.

Mike was gazing at a point somewhere in the middle of the table. His voice was expressionless.

"I suppose so."

Suzy gave his hand an extra squeeze.

"That's very noble of you, Mike. I won't be any trouble. Maybe I can help you with the cooking."

Afterwards Suzy told me she thought I'd been horribly insensitive to make such a proposal at that moment, but it just seemed the obvious thing to do. And although she ticked me off properly about it, she seemed quite prepared to go along with the idea. She moved some of her stuff into the flat, but she left most of it at the place she'd been sharing with her girlfriend. She went back there from time to time. Obviously the new arrangement solved a lot of problems for the two of us. It also meant that Mike would get to see a lot more of Suzy, although not nearly as much of her as I was seeing.

*

The five thousand I'd paid into my bank account would keep the wolves from the door, but there was no suggestion that we were going to stop there. We'd learned quite a bit from hitting the post offices and we felt confident enough now to embark on a series of raids on bank counters. That meant visiting different branches and looking at their general layout and suitability. They all needed to be branches like Suzy's, where the counters weren't overlooked from behind by open-plan offices or in a direct line of vision from the street. Mike had finished his course and exams so he could help me in the mornings as well as the afternoons. We couldn't do anything after the banks had closed to customers, of course, so we'd return to the flat and compare notes. That way we were always there before Suzy got back from work. Mike would already be doing something about preparing dinner, unless we were eating out, which we could afford to do more often these days.

One evening Suzy was very late, and Mike didn't know what to do about the dinner. He put a saucepan of water on to boil and cut up the vegetables, then he looked at his watch, shook his head, and turned out the light under the saucepan. He paced around the kitchen for a bit with his hands in his pockets and then he put some salt in the water, ground some herbs to powder, chopped the parsley even finer and went back to pacing. I must say it wasn't like her at all; if there was some delay she would usually let us know. When she did finally show up she was talking before she was even through the door.

"That Mr. Meredrew is a such a swine! Everything has to be done his way down to the last detail and if you leave out the tiniest thing, he talks to you as if he's at the limit of his patience." She put down her bag and took her jacket off, still talking. "He had a go at me *twice* yesterday and this afternoon he went and *fired* Lynsey. She's absolutely *desperate*. She's expecting a baby in September! Caroline thinks it was because of her maternity leave coming up. To dismiss her like that! She'll *never* get another job without a decent reference. I got in touch with the Union representative. He saw us straight away. He said there was a good case for showing constructive dismissal or sexual discrimination. He said if the bank won't reinstate her they'll go to tribunal. At least she should get her job back, probably at another branch. That calmed her down a bit. Caroline's taken her home. She's such a star." She scooped back her thick hair. "Phew, what a mess! Sorry, that's why I'm so late."

Mike made the dinner, and I washed up, and we sat down together at the kitchen table while Suzy prepared the coffee. Mike was more relaxed now that dinner was over but he looked thoughtful, so I said nothing. As soon as Suzy had set out the coffee and sat down, Mike said:

"Look, I've had an idea. I think I know how we can settle Meredrew's hash, good and proper. Anyone interested?"

26

I looked up quickly. So did Suzy.

"What, play a sort of trick on him, you mean?" she asked.

"Something like that, but I'm not talking about anything trivial. He'd be off your back for a long time, maybe for good."

"Gosh, that would be wonderful."

"Rodge?"

"Are you kidding? More than anything I would love to stick it to that bastard," I said.

My reaction would come as no surprise to Suzy; she already knew there was no love lost between me and her manager.

"It'll take about two weeks for Rodge and I to set it up. We're going to need a little help from you as well, Suzy."

"What sort of help?" she asked guardedly.

"Well, to start with I need to establish people's movements. Let me ask you something. Money from the counters has to be returned to a safe overnight, for security, right?"

She said nothing, so he continued.

"In the morning, someone has to open the safe and money has to be transferred to the counter positions for the day's trading. I would guess all that happens well before the bank opens at nine o'clock. So who opens the safe, and who transfers the money, and when does that happen?"

She stared at him wide-eyed.

"Mike," she said, "do you realize what you're asking? Staff

are sworn to secrecy about things like that; it's part of our contract. I could lose my job!"

"Well, Rodge and I will be taking much bigger risks than that. I guess it just depends how much you want to get rid of Meredrew."

I could see that she was in a bit of a quandary. I wasn't sure what scheme Mike had in mind but the mere thought of that self-important sod of a manager getting it in the neck made me yearn for Suzy to commit herself to it.

Eventually she said: "If things went wrong, would anyone know I'd helped you?"

"Not a chance."

"Really, Mike? I'm serious."

"Really."

"Well, all right. The assistant manager opens the safe. Actually more often than not it's the senior customer service officer."

"Who's the senior customer service officer?"

"Lynsey. Well, it used to be Lynsey. Now that she's gone… well, I suppose it'll be me. I'm the next in line, and I've done it quite often, when people have been on holiday or ill or such-like. I'll be acting up till they promote me."

"Is the manager around at that time?"

"Oh no, he usually gets in about nine. We open the street door at nine whether he's in or not."

"So what time do you get in?"

"About eight-fifteen. Gives me time to hang my coat up, get settled, have a cup of tea. Then I go to the safe to pick up my till. I'm responsible for my own till. It's the same for the other girls on the counter."

"That would be around eight-thirty?"

"Normally, yes."

"What do you mean by 'normally'?"

"Well on a Friday we generally start earlier. Friday's a busy day. There are queues of people waiting to be paid so we're tied up with customers pretty much all day. At our branch we like to bring the book-keeping up to date before the weekend. So we get the counters ready and then the staff work on the journal roll. We get as far as we can before nine."

"And that's done in an office round the back somewhere?"

"Yes."

"And everyone's involved in this, what from eight-thirty to nine?"

"Yes."

"Okay. Now there are three tellers. Do you have keys to all three tills?"

"No, of course not. Only my own."

"But there must be spares. Where are they kept?"

"Mike, that's confidential…"

"Okay, Suzy, I don't need to know where they're kept. Just tell me if you have access to them."

She looked at him for a moment, then said "yes" very quietly, as if she didn't want to be heard.

"Good. Excellent. Now, the next thing I need to know is, where does the manager live?"

Suzy looked at him in alarm. "Mike, I don't like the sound of this…"

"Don't worry. Look, if he lives outside London it's no big deal anyway. I'll have to base the plan on his office. But it wouldn't be nearly as effective."

"I do have his telephone number. I need to have it in case of emergencies."

Suzy opened her handbag, took out a small leather address

book and leafed through it. "Here we are. Well, it's an 0208 number so it should be London."

"Is he ex-directory?"

"I don't know."

"Let's look him up then."

Mike booted up the laptop, and I mooched over to watch the screen with him. He logged on to the server and brought up the Directory Enquiries web site. Reading off the screen, he muttered, "Surname or Business," and typed MEREDREW. "Area", he said, and typed LONDON. Then he clicked on the search button marked PEOPLE. After a moment or two a list of Meredrews came up.

"What's his initials?" he asked Suzy.

"M.H. It's Morton something."

He scrolled down the names.

"This looks like it might be it."

He clicked the GO button at the side of the name and up came an address and telephone number.

"Suzy, have a look. Is that the number, there?"

Suzy came over with her little address book to check the screen.

"Yes, that's it."

She went and sat down again.

Mike scribbled the address on a scrap of paper. I pointed to a button below the address, labelled SEE MAP DETAILS.

"Oh yes," he said quietly. "Do let's have a map."

He clicked the button and a very pixellated map formed on the screen and increased in resolution.

"Ah, it's Richmond." Half turning to me he said under his voice, "This is too easy."

He disconnected from the server and we sat down again.

"Suzy," he said. "While we're about it, do you have a

number for the manager of the Security Division of your bank? Not an internal number; I need one in the public domain."

"I can get hold of one."

"Good. And I need a large envelope, the type of thing you'd use to put money or documents in a safe deposit. Preferably something with the bank's name on it."

"Okay, I can get that for you easy enough."

"Great."

"Is that it?"

"That's it. Well nearly it—there's just one more thing. We'll schedule this for a Friday; let's see, it'll be two weeks from this Friday. That Friday morning I'd like you to pick up the spare set of till keys."

Suzy's eyes had gone wide and dark, but Mike continued breezily.

"When you all go off to do the book-keeping, I'd like you to hang back and open the three tills. Gap them a tiny bit, just so as the lock's not engaged. Then put the keys back where you found them."

Suzy's mouth was open.

"Mike! You're not serious! I can't do that! I'm not doing that!"

"Suzy, Suzy, calm down. Look, it won't even be noticed. I guarantee that by the time the girls come back to the counter all those drawers will be locked again."

"Oh, and precisely how...?"

"Now don't ask me that. It's better you don't know. But it'll happen. I guarantee."

"You guarantee. You guarantee I'll lose my job, that's what you guarantee! This is ridiculous! I've said far too much already. There's too much at stake. I'm a trusted employee, for God's sake. Forget it! I'm not doing it."

Mike threw up his open hands.

"Okay, that's it, then. We can't do it. Sorry. Lynsey gets the sack and you'll have to live with your lovely manager."

Suzy bit her lip and said nothing.

I didn't know where all this had been leading but since it had obviously run into a brick wall I thought it was time I stepped in.

"Mike, can I get this straight? You want Suzy to get us a phone number and a big bank envelope. And that's not a problem, Suzy?"

She shrugged petulantly.

"But you also want her to borrow the spare keys, just temporarily, and leave the till drawers unlocked, just temporarily."

"That's right," Mike replied. "I wouldn't have asked her if we could do it any other way. I didn't think it was that big a deal. No one's going to notice and when it's all over there'll be absolutely nothing to connect her with it." He turned to Suzy. "I'm telling you, Suzy, if you do this, we can really sock it to Meredrew. You don't, we can't. It's as simple as that."

Suzy was shaking her head. "I've no idea what you're up to, Mike…"

"I know. And I'm not spelling it out because I don't want to involve you any more than I absolutely have to. Sorry and all that, but I need those three drawers left unlocked for about ten minutes, that's all, and I can't see any other way of doing it except to ask you. Rodge and I will do everything else. Won't we, Rodge?"

"Er, yes, of course," I said, not having a clue what he was talking about.

"See, Rodge and I will do the rest. But this is your bit."

Suzy looked over at me. "Rodger…?"

I knew she was appealing to me to back her up. Instead I hoped my expression was conveying what I was thinking. *Please do this, Suzy. I know it's a lot to ask but please do it.*

There was a long silence. Suzy looked away, staring vacantly, resting her forehead on her fingertips and massaging nervously above one eyebrow. Then she said huskily:

"All right. But if anything goes wrong I'll never speak to either of you again."

And she got up suddenly and stormed out of the room.

Mike and I looked at each other. I heaved a sigh of relief. Mike smiled.

"We'll go over the details tomorrow," he whispered.

27

We'd already identified two banks that were suitable, and we spent the rest of that week scouting around to bring the number up to six. In each branch we took GPS and ultrasonic distance readings in the usual way so we could be sure I'd land in a good position behind the counter. We did the same for the Cromwell Road branch where Suzy worked. And then we were all set. On the following Tuesday we went into action.

Mike roused me at six-thirty. It's not in my nature to get up so early, and I detest having to do it, but timing was going to be crucial to this whole operation. All these branches had several tellers. If I let them get in place before I arrived behind the counter I wouldn't be able to control all of them; there was a real risk that one would hit a concealed panic button, sounding the alarm and alerting the police. The only way to avoid this was to get there before the first teller came in.

We walked over to the Department and warmed up the equipment. When everything was stable Mike projected me to the first target. I had my gun and I was wearing the balaclava, now dyed black. I just waited there quietly. There was no need to conceal myself; all the activity was going on somewhere in the rooms behind, and no one could see me from the street. It was eight-fifteen.

Seventeen minutes later a girl came in with her till drawer.

I covered her mouth with my hand and jammed the barrel of the gun against her forehead. I wasn't gentle; she had to know I meant business. I pointed the barrel at her till and then at my duffel bag and hissed, "Put it all in." Then I pressed the cold muzzle of the gun hard behind her ear and kept it there while she did it. When she'd transferred all the money I told her to lie face down on the floor and not to move or make a sound. She was still lying there when I did my disappearing act.

We did two more targets the same way, one on Wednesday morning and one on Thursday morning. We skipped Friday and Monday and went into action again the following Tuesday and Wednesday. I'd only netted about thirty thousand pounds so far but that wasn't to be sniffed at. In any case this was just the prelude to the main part of the plan; that would go into action on Friday morning when we hit Suzy's branch. Meanwhile we had just one more job to do, on the Thursday morning.

And that's when it all went pear-shaped.

I was at the target at eight-fifteen in the morning, as before. The teller who came in first was a slim woman in her thirties. She didn't see me and I moved behind her as usual, clapped my hand over her mouth, brandished the gun, and signalled for her to put the money in the bag. I'd done this so many times now it seemed almost routine. But this girl had other ideas. She just dropped the till drawer and stamped her high heel down on my instep. The pain stabbed up my leg like a white-hot lance. I cried out; I couldn't help it. I must have loosened my grip because she whirled round and tried to scratch my eyes out. I jerked back but her fingers caught in the slit in my balaclava and dragged it down, her long nails raking my cheeks. At the same time she started to scream at the top of her lungs. The noise was unbelievable. I shoved her hard in the chest and she fell backwards against the counter but right away she was fumbling frantically for something underneath it. Before she could find the alarm button I backhanded her with the gun. It caught her a good wallop on the side of her forehead and she staggered. Then I brought the butt of the gun down hard on the top of her head and she folded and dropped to the floor.

My breathing was so loud in my ears I thought the whole world must be able to hear. I looked around quickly. The phone on her counter had a long cable—that would do nicely. I snatched it up and wound the ends round my hands. Then I heard doors opening and urgent voices coming from the back. I hesitated, standing over her with the cable taut between my hands, the phone still swinging and twisting at one end. Now there were running footsteps. It was too late. I gave Mike the signal and I was back in the cage. I dropped the empty bag and walked out of the cage, pulling off the balaclava.

Mike must have taken in the empty bag and my manner in a single glance.

"What's the matter? What happened?" he said.

"We've got a problem. Bloody woman had a go at me. Stamped on my foot and scratched my face. I smacked her around a bit but she screamed so bloody loud the others started coming and I had to call a halt. Really hurt me, stupid cow."

I passed my fingers gingerly over my face, expecting them to come away covered in blood. There was nothing.

Mike looked at me quizzically. "There's not a mark on you, Rodge."

"Come to think of it, my foot's not hurting any more,

either." I tapped the floor lightly with the foot. Then I stamped it down hard. "That's not the point, though, is it? She got a look at me!"

"How much of a look?"

"Well, she dragged my balaclava down. She's seen the bottom half of my face."

Mike shrugged.

"Mike, this is serious! The cops'll get her to identify me! They'll get a drawing made. They'll have her looking through footage from the security cameras. She'll recognize me!"

Mike was shaking his head. "The security cameras cover the other side of the counter, Rodge."

"I know, but I was the one who cased that branch. They'll publish a photo, and it'll be in all the newspapers and someone will recognize me—Ledsham, or that bloody manager, or one of the idiots from our year—"

"Rodge—"

"I should have dealt with her then and there. I would have done, too, but there wasn't time. I've got to go back, Mike. In person, I mean. Forget the operation tomorrow. This takes precedence. I've got to follow her."

"What for?"

"She's got to be silenced."

"You mean killed?"

"Unless you know of another way."

"Rodge, the idea was robbery, plain and simple. You've already made it robbery with violence—"

"I couldn't help—"

"I know, all right. But murder? Forget it. It's not happening, Rodge. Not on my beat."

"It's all very well for you, Mike. It isn't your face that'll be plastered all over the newspapers."

"Rodge, will you calm down? Let's look at this objectively. Put your balaclava on and show me exactly what she did."

I glared at him but did as he asked. I hooked my fingers in the slit and brought it down about level with my mouth. He gave a short laugh.

"For Chrissake, Rodge! Your own mother couldn't recognize you again from that much. I certainly couldn't."

"The security video—"

"The camera's trained just in front of the counter, Rodge. If it picked you up at all when you cased the branch you'll be a small figure somewhere in the background, apparently making a phone call. There's no way she could recognize you again from that. And that's assuming they haven't recorded over it by now. Now, you said you hit her. Where? How hard?"

I thought about it, seeing for a moment the crumpled body, blood streaming from the right side of her head where I hit her the first time. The second blow had been heavier. I know I hit her as hard as I could but I wasn't at my usual strength and the gun was only half its normal weight.

"On the head," I said quietly. "Quite hard."

"Did you knock her out?"

"Yes."

He grimaced. "Okay. By now, that branch will be crawling with police. In a few more minutes they'll be loading her into an ambulance and carting her off to hospital—probably the A & E at Charing Cross."

"I'll go there, then—"

"Will you wait a moment? Now listen. She's a material witness so they'll certainly give her a police escort. They'll have a quiet word with someone and she'll be whisked away to a private room with a police guard on the door."

"If we found out where, you could project me—"

"Let me finish. You say you knocked her out. She's got concussion. In all probability she'll have no memory whatever of what happened in the few minutes before you hit her. Even if she does remember, she hasn't seen enough of you to be able to recognize you again. At some stage, forensic may scrape under her fingernails. They won't find anything there either because every bit of you came back together when we killed the resonance, including the skin and blood she scraped off your face. So, Rodge," he said it slowly, with heavy emphasis, "what in fuck's name are you worried about?"

I bit my lip. Mike was still looking at me, one eyebrow raised. It was easier for him to think logically; he hadn't just been through what I'd been through. That's why I'd over-reacted. Normally I wouldn't have let him take charge of me like that. I took a deep breath and expelled it slowly.

"All right."

"Now listen, Rodge." His voice was more conciliatory. "Let's not take our eye off the ball. We've put a lot of effort into this. We're ready to roll. All we need to do is hit Suzy's branch tomorrow morning. It'll be nice and easy. They'll all be round the back, doing the book-keeping, so there's no risk of something like this happening again. Now, are you up for it or not?"

I considered it for a moment. It was true I'd lost sight of the bigger picture. The important thing was to make sure that slime Meredrew was well and truly shafted. Nothing must deflect me from that.

"It shook me up a bit, Mike, that's all. I'm all right now."

"So we're going in as planned?"

"Yes."

"Good man. Tomorrow's the day we put the final pieces in place."

28

The "string of daring bank robberies" had hit the national press by now, and of course they'd all been talking about it in the bank. Suzy was quite excited when she came home that evening. They'd been told to tighten up on security, but everyone was focusing on points of entry, of course, so it didn't affect our plan in the slightest. Suzy didn't seem to connect the robberies with us. That wasn't surprising. Her imagination would never have stretched to the sort of technology Mike and I were using, and she wouldn't have guessed in a million years that her two nice flatmates were a couple of hold-up artists.

She'd brought home a *Daily Telegraph* and Mike and I had a quick look through it while she was changing out of her working clothes. The news coverage of the robberies was brief and factual but there was some additional comment in one of the columns, written in a faintly humorous vein. It ended:

…What the police and everyone else will be wondering is: why? Why set up an elaborate armed robbery, with all the risks involved, for the comparatively small amount of money in a bank till? It's possible the thieves thought they would get away with more. If so this must be one of the most incompetent gangs in criminal history.

Mike gave a derisive laugh but I was irritated.

"Who the hell are they are calling incompetent?" I demanded.

"Shh, Rodge!" he hissed. "Don't let Suzy hear you. Look, don't take any notice of these idiots. They're treating it like a conventional crime. They've got no idea what they're dealing with."

We worked on Suzy again that evening, making sure she understood precisely what she had to do the following morning and how important it was. She soon lost patience with us.

"For God's sake, you two, will you stop treating me like some kind of idiot! I said I'll do it and I'll do it. I don't know why I did, and it's against my better judgement, but I said I would, and I will. Now, leave me alone!"

We left her alone.

*

In the morning we were out of the flat before she was, but she would see nothing unusual in that. Mike had already covered it by pretending to complain about my long-winded experiments.

At the lab we switched on the equipment and went through what we'd come to refer to as our "flight checks". By eight-thirty I was in the cage with the duffel bag. I gave Mike the nod.

The moment I landed behind the counter I could see that Suzy had done her stuff: all three till drawers were very slightly open. I transferred the money in the drawers to my duffel bag, being careful to close each drawer afterwards. It took just a few minutes and nobody saw me. I gave the signal and I was back in the lab.

We took the money out of the bag and dropped it straight into the bank safe deposit envelope that Suzy had got for us. I was about to lick the flap to seal it down when Mike stopped me.

"Don't lick it. Forensic may be able to analyse the saliva."

"So what?"

"They'll check it against Meredrew's, and it won't match."

"Ah, I see what you mean. What then? Sellotape?"

"No, it'll take fingerprints. Use tap water—here, use a tissue to wet the flap. Okay, now stick it down."

Next we set the coordinates for Meredrew's house. We'd put in some preparation for this bit. I'd been down there once, by public transport, at night. I found it easily enough. It was a typical suburban house in a row of typical suburban houses. It was certainly a far cry from my family home. I remember standing there on the pavement, thinking that this pathetic life style must be what bank managers aspire to. I had the GPS receiver and ultrasonic tape measure in my pocket and it only took a moment or two to record the position and the compass reading and the distance from where I was standing to the front bay. Later I added a couple of metres to extend the distance into the front room and we had the coordinates for the projection.

Mike had also been down there the two previous Fridays, getting there early in the morning to watch the house. The routine was the same each time. The manager left for work at eight sharp, carrying a briefcase. He was obviously walking to the Underground. At eight-thirty the automatic garage door opened and a car backed out. Mike said it was a Mercedes 4X4. The garage door closed and the car drove off. He said there was a driver and a passenger, both women he thought, but he couldn't see them clearly. It was probably Meredrew's wife doing the school run because at nine o'clock the car returned with just the driver. Based on that information we thought it would be best if I arrived there at nine-thirty. Risky as it was, I had to do this thing with someone in the house; otherwise the burglar alarm would be set.

So at nine-thirty I was standing in the cage again, equipped as usual except that this time I was wearing a pair of rubber gloves to make sure I didn't leave any fingerprints behind. Mike pressed the button and I landed smack in the middle of Meredrew's front room. It was sparsely furnished as an occasional lounge. A couple of soft armchairs and a sofa were arranged on three sides of a glass coffee table. They faced a gas simulated coal fire set in a tiled fireplace with a mirror over it. The mirror reflected a not-very-good oil painting on the opposite wall. Under the painting there was a sideboard with a dried flower arrangement in a crystal glass vase and some photographs in frames. I strolled over and glanced at the photos without much interest. One was a portrait of a girl of about twelve—his daughter, probably. The next was a black-and-white wedding picture of Meredrew with his bride. The last was a colour photo, a bit faded, of the three of them on holiday somewhere. The daughter was a bit younger then. I looked away—the mere sight of him turned my stomach. This room was presumably used for entertaining. I found it hard to imagine that Meredrew had any friends. Perhaps they were just as odious as he was. More likely it was his wife who had the friends and they had to put up with him. I was wasting time: this room was clearly unsuitable for my purposes.

Somewhere not far away I could hear sounds of movement. I opened the door carefully and peeked out. To the right was the entrance hall and the front door. To the left, towards the back of the house, was a short corridor, at the end of which a door was open. The noises seemed to be coming from in there. I crept towards it. I could see a counter-top, cupboards, and a stone-flagged floor. Clearly this was the kitchen or breakfast room. A sudden noise made me jump; then I realized it was a dishwasher starting up. Immediately to my left was another door. It creaked slightly as I opened it but I didn't think that would be audible over the steady purr of that dishwasher. I put my head round the door; the room was empty. I went in.

It was a sitting-room with a French window to the garden. There was a television and a small stereo system, with speakers in the corners. On the wall there was a set of mahogany shelves, which were stacked with books, videotapes and CDs. It was perfect. I opened the duffel bag, took out the brown envelope with the money, reached up to the top shelf, and tucked it in behind some large books. Then I stepped back to make sure it wasn't visible. It wasn't.

My job was finished. I transferred my awareness back to the cage and signalled for Mike to detune and power down.

"Well done, Rodge." Mike greeted me. "All okay?"

"Yes. Shame to leave all that money there, though."

"But worth it."

"Every penny."

"Well, there's only one thing more to do and you can't do that till tomorrow morning so you may as well relax."

*

We switched off all the equipment and returned to the flat. Mike bought a *Daily Telegraph* as we were walking back and we looked through it while we were having our coffee. There was an account of the violent attack on a bank teller the previous morning, which had left the victim unconscious. A statement from the hospital said the woman was suffering from serious head injuries, but that she was now recovering from her ordeal. Her condition was given as "comfortable". My guess was that it was anything but.

Mike's voice was flat. He said, "No funny remarks in that column today, I notice. Suddenly it's no longer a laughing matter."

"She'll be all right."

"It shouldn't have happened, Rodge."

I tried to steer him away.

"They seem quite certain this robbery was connected with the others," I said, "but it looks like that's just their opinion. The police spokesman says they're 'keeping an open mind'."

"He would say that. A policeman always keeps an open mind when he doesn't have anything to put in it. I'll tell you something though, Rodge. The banks are going to be taking this a whole lot more seriously now. A few thousand missing from the till is one thing but this is quite another. It's not their money they'll be worrying about; they're going to have a big job on, trying to reassure their employees and their insurance companies. I bet every branch will get extra security and they'll have their guards making the rounds of the premises each morning before the staff come to the counters. Whatever else you've done, clobbering that woman yesterday has put paid to this kind of caper for the foreseeable future."

"Well then, it's lucky we finished in time."

*

The following morning I phoned the manager of the Bank's Security Division. I used a soft Irish accent. His secretary tried to block me but I wasn't having any. Eventually she said she'd see if he could speak to me and shortly after that there was a click and he came on the line.

"Cubbins. Can I help you?"

He sounded irritated, as if helping anyone was the last thing on his mind.

"I wanted to have a word with you about these bank robberies the last two weeks, sir. I have some information I think will interest you."

"Oh yes?" He sounded mildly interested. "Who am I speaking to, please?"

"I'm sorry, I can't tell you that. D'ye want the information or not?"

"Go on," he said cautiously.

"For all I know, sir, some of these robberies were the genuine article, sir, but I'm thinkin' this last one on Friday was not that at all."

"Oh? Why do you say that?"

"Last evenin' I was at a house in Richmond. Doesn't matter what I was doin' there so don't ask me that if ye don't mind. Now it so happens the house belongs to that there manager chappie from the bank in Cromwell Road."

"And…?"

"And didn't I see him, sir, with a very large amount of money?" I pronounced "large" as "lairge". I was really getting into this. "Stuffin' it into a brown envelope he was. A very large amount of money indeed. And he put it behind a bookshelf, so he did."

"And you saw him do this?"

"That I did, sir."

"Behind a bookshelf?"

"Yes, sir."

"So what?"

"Ah, well that's what I thought meself, sir, until I heard the news this mornin' about the robbery at his bank. And I was thinkin' how convenient it might be if he removed that money hisself, and only pretended it was a robbery. It seemed like an awful big coincidence to me now."

"Well coincidence or not—who did you say you were?"

"I'm not tellin' you that, sir, for me own good reasons, and begging your pardon if you ax me again I'll have to put this here phone down."

"Well, what do you expect me to do?"

"Well, you might go down this day and ax the gentlemen if he keeps large amounts of money at his house. And if he says he does not, you'll know what to do now, won't you? And you and your people will have quite a success on their hands."

"I can't do that. The man's a branch manager. The company trusts him completely. I'm not ready to ransack his house on an… some anonymous tip-off."

"Well, sir, now that's for you to be decidin'. But I know what I saw with my two eyes and if you don't do some investigatin' then I'll have to contact the police, and then it'll be out of your hands. And when it all comes out I think your company might want to know why you didn't do sump'n' about it yerself."

There was a pause as this sank in.

"Where are you speaking from?"

I put the phone down. "That's enough of that," I said in my normal voice.

Mike was grinning at me. I grinned back. I thought I'd

done quite a good job of the accent. I had cousins in County Mayo, and I holidayed with them for a few weeks when I was about twelve. I never forgot the lovely music of the local accent.

"Do you think he took the bait?" Mike asked.

"Yes, I think so. He's ponderous but he's not stupid."

"They're going to wonder who this Irish, or fake-Irish, gent is, and how he came to see what went on."

"Yes, but only afterwards. If they find that envelope we've stitched him up properly. They'll drive themselves mad about the anonymous tipster but the evidence is solid, so it won't change anything. Mike, should we tell Suzy about any of this?"

"No," Mike said quickly. "Don't breathe a word of it. The less she knows the safer it will be—for her and for us."

29

On Monday, Suzy came back from work brimming with excitement.

"Guess what!" she said. "Mr. Meredrew's been suspended! Isn't it fantastic?"

Rodge and I made "fancy that" kind of noises.

Suzy looked at us and her eyes narrowed.

"You did this, didn't you? How did you do it?"

I opened my mouth but Mike got in first.

"Trust me on this one, Suzy, it's better if you don't know. Who's taken his place?"

"Owen Hughes is acting up; he was assistant manager."

She was still eyeing us suspiciously.

"I think I met him once," I said, trying to divert her from asking more. "Is he a bit portly? Has one of those lovely melodious Welsh voices?"

"That's right, that's him. Totally different personality to Meredrew. Still efficient but much more laid back. He likes to give people responsibility. All the staff like him. He'll probably get the job permanently."

Suzy was on cloud nine for the rest of the week but when she came home the following Monday she was in an altogether more sombre mood. She had a newspaper folded back to an article, which she shoved at us. I sat down to read it, with Mike looking over my shoulder.

BANK MANAGER DIES

Morton Meredrew, former manager of the Cromwell Road branch of the National Central Bank, was found dead yesterday at his home in Richmond. The police are not looking for anyone else in connection with the incident.

Mr. Meredrew was relieved of his duties at the bank a week ago pending the outcome of criminal proceedings on charges of embezzlement. He had been released on bail.

It is alleged that Mr. Meredrew took advantage of the recent spate of thefts from bank counters in London to stage a similar occurrence at his own bank. The money, still in a sealed envelope, was recovered from his home. Mr. Meredrew has always protested that he did not know how it got there, but was unable to account for the absence of any signs of a break-in, either at the bank or at his home.

A spokesman for the bank said: "This is a tragic turn of events. Mr. Meredrew was a long-standing employee of the Bank and an extremely conscientious manager. The behaviour of which he was accused was totally out of character. Staff at his branch have confirmed that Mr. Meredrew had been showing evidence of stress over the last few weeks. Our sincere sympathies go out to his family."

Mr. Meredrew leaves a wife and teenage daughter.

"I feel just awful," said Suzy, sitting down heavily. "I mean, I didn't like the man one little bit and I was really glad he was suspended, but suicide! It's such a dreadful thing to happen. And he had a *family*."

Mike and I murmured our agreement. In actual fact I could have whooped for joy. It had come out even better than I hoped. I hadn't expected him to go that far, but I had no more regrets than if I'd crushed a particularly repulsive insect under my foot. I guess Mike didn't sound too convincing either. Suzy glared at us.

"How could you do such a thing?" she demanded.

Her big brown eyes had gone very liquid and it looked to me like she was going to cry. Mike had obviously picked up the warning signs too.

"Come on, be fair, Suzy," he said. "All we did was play a trick on him. We couldn't have known he was going to top himself now, could we?"

She blinked rapidly. He put an arm round her shoulders, a gesture that made me bristle a bit, but I kept quiet.

"Come on," he said. "We can't do anything about it, can we? It's not going to help to get all upset. Try and put it out of your mind. Look, I was going to cook something good tonight. Please don't spoil it."

She pouted. "Maybe I can help. What were you going to make?"

Her voice was shaky. I thought the tears still weren't all that far away. However, Mike seemed to be in a buoyant mood.

"I'm-a maka for you the e-special dinner," he said in a cod Italian accent. "I cook-a for you the Spaghetti a la Frutti di Mare—mwuh!"

He held his finger and thumb together and kissed them

in an extravagant gesture. I'd never seen him in such high spirits. Suzy was trying to smother a little smile, but Mike was prancing about, planting a bottle of Chianti Classico Riserva on the table and extolling its virtues in that same excruciating accent. Then he whirled an apron around his head before putting it on with a flourish. I had to laugh myself. Suzy was soon drawn in and started to help Mike with the cooking.

"Can I do anything?" I was feeling a bit useless.

"Yes," Mike said. "You open the wine, Rodge. Pour a glass for the three of us. We can have it as an aperitif. And while you're about it put some in this cup; I'll use it in the cooking. And then if you could lay the table that would be a help. Spoons and forks. And don't forget water. Suzy likes a glass of water."

I have to say the dinner was fantastic. Mike knew that Suzy wasn't all that keen on shellfish, so he'd used a mixture of other fish and put in generous amounts of oregano and red wine. To top it off he tore up a few leaves of fresh basil. It tasted every bit as good as it looked. The Chianti was a cracker too; it went down like velvet.

Throughout the meal Mike kept us entertained. When it came to dessert time he smacked his forehead in mock anguish and exclaimed:

"I'm-a nearly forgot-a the gelato!"

He dived into the fridge and a few moments later served up vanilla ice-cream with a chocolate sauce, sprinkled with chopped roasted almonds. His energy seemed limitless. When he served the coffees and sat down I think both Suzy and I were expecting the entertainment to continue. Instead there was a sudden change of mood. In his normal, matter-of-fact voice he said:

"Now, boys and girls. Who would like to be seriously rich?"

SUSAN

30

Mike was so funny when he was doing the Italian restaurateur act. I know Mummy and Daddy would have liked him. It's true he was a bit rudderless, career-wise. But he was bright—even if he did try to play the ordinary Essex boy—and he had a good degree and work experience. Mummy would probably have said, "All he needs, dear, is a good woman behind him. You mark my words, he'll make a good husband and father." Only I didn't want a husband and father. Not yet.

Not that Mummy and Daddy were at all anxious to see me married. If anything they'd have been happier if I was still living at home, where they could keep an eye on me. It's just as well I'm not; I think I'd have gone insane by now. I mean, I understand about Amy and everything, but it wasn't my fault, was it? I don't even remember what she looked like. But then, I was only five when she died. All I can remember is feeling resentful about all the attention they lavished on her. It got worse towards the end, with Amy in bed most of the time. I didn't know what was going on and I couldn't understand why they wouldn't let me see her. And afterwards they wouldn't talk about it or keep any photos around the house—I suppose the memories were just too raw for them. So I forgot what she looked like. Isn't that awful? Your own sister!

After Amy had "gone to Heaven", as they put it, I was an

only child and I became the focus of their lives. I was so precious to them I couldn't sneeze without Mummy thinking it was "the start of something". When I first started to have periods I had a bit of pain with it. Mummy promptly tucked me up in bed and insisted on a doctor coming to see me. Not a male doctor, either—she wasn't haven't any men lay their hands on *her* daughter—no, it had to be a female doctor. Of course, she diagnosed it right away and prescribed something, but that wasn't enough for Mummy. I listened to the doctor talking to her outside my room.

"It's only a touch of dysmenorrhoea, Mrs. Whittingham. Nothing to worry about."

"You don't understand," Mummy was almost hissing the words. "There's a family history…" And then she brought herself to say something, but so quietly I couldn't hear it. "Her sister died of it! With all due respect, I think I should have a second opinion."

"Well, I can refer her if you like, Mrs. Whittingham, but I've examined her thoroughly and I can assure you she's a perfectly healthy girl. I do understand your anxiety, but I think you've got to consider the effect of all that investigation on Susan. You don't want to make an invalid of her now, do you? I tell you what. Have her take the medication I've prescribed. If it hasn't improved in a few days we'll reassess the situation. Is that all right?"

It cleared up, of course, just like all the other near-death experiences I had. I know they meant it for my good, but heavens—what a stifling atmosphere to grow up in!

I could hardly wait to go to university. Even then they'd come to visit me and they'd fuss over my digs, and worry about how I looked, and ask me what I was eating. And then, after I graduated, Costa Rica! That was the best! Real freedom at last, for three whole months! And of course there was Raoul. Everyone in the party must have guessed what was going on but nobody said anything. We had such a great time.

After I got back there was no way I could settle down at home again—it just wouldn't have worked. It wasn't Daddy so much—he seemed all right now— but Mummy still found it hard to relinquish control of me. And then I'd have felt so trapped socially, being eyed by all the pimply young men I'd been at school with. I wanted to go somewhere that was so huge I could really get lost in it. So I enrolled for a PGCE course at a college in the East End of London. I suppose I was asking for trouble and I got it: an inner city school with every problem in the book. It was a nightmare—I couldn't get out fast enough. That was when I joined the Bank.

I'm pretty much where I want to be for the moment; I've got a steady job and I share a flat with Siobhan. So I've achieved my independence. It was hard enough to get it. I'm not going to give it up so easily.

Poor Mike. That first time he came to the Bank and asked me out for a coffee he looked like a puppy waiting at a table, hoping someone would throw him a bone. Well, it was nice to have someone to go out with, someone not too demanding, and he was good company, but I didn't want anything more out of it than that. I told him I'd just come out of a long-term relationship and that it had hurt me badly. Actually I was being a bit economical with the truth. I'd had plenty of relationships but none of them had lasted very long and it was always me who broke them off. He was very sweet about it, though. One time he cooked a nice meal for me, with my favourite wine and everything. He really went to a lot of trouble. I should have been more grateful. The trouble was, the more he tried to please me, the more it turned me off.

Rodger was a totally different proposition. Mike had told me a lot about him; he was obviously in awe of Rodger because he was so clever. I'd formed a mental picture of his friend: he'd be a short nerdy fellow with horn-rimmed glasses, a pasty complexion, and a lot of hair in need of a good wash and comb. And then in walks this Adonis! I mean, what a dish! Tall, blond hair curling onto his forehead, and these two creases, like long dimples, running down either side of his jaw. Mike introduced me and he said hallo in a perfunctory sort of way, and then just ignored me. After a while he went off to another room. It wasn't often men walked away from me like that. I felt quite disappointed.

To get him back in my orbit I suggested we went out as a threesome. I know Mike wasn't that keen but he couldn't very well say no. Soon we were going out together all the time. Mike didn't like having to share me with Rodger and he'd have a fit of the sulks, and that left Rodger and me doing a lot of the talking.

Then, one evening, Rodger put his hand on my thigh. There was nothing surreptitious about it, not the furtive fingers creeping under my skirt that some boys had tried in the cinema after the lights had gone down. He was talking about something with Mike at the time. Under the table he just brushed my skirt up and placed his hand around my thigh. It was so proprietorial, it was like we'd been married for twenty years, for God's sake! I couldn't believe his nerve. I clapped my legs together tightly so he couldn't do anything more. I could feel the heat of his big hand on the inside of my thigh, and I realized I was breathing fast, through my nose. Rodger didn't react; he just carried on his conversation with Mike, and Mike hadn't noticed a thing. After a while I relaxed a little. You could say I was wondering what he'd do, but if I'm honest I know jolly well what I wanted him to do. He just patted me and took his hand away. All this time he never stopped talking to Mike. That was Rodger all over: he'd always do what you didn't want, and wouldn't do what you did want.

When Mike was revising for his exams Rodger and I went out on our own. Siobhan, my flatmate, had gone back to her parents' place in Ireland for a few days, so the flat was empty and I invited him back for a coffee. He didn't wait for coffee; he just took me into the bedroom and started to undress me. I said:

"Rodger, I don't want this."

"Of course you do," he replied, in a matter-of-fact way.

He was right. Of course I did.

Raoul was good, but then Raoul was my first, so I had no one to compare him with. The ones I'd had in London didn't even register. Rodger was in another league. Raoul used his tongue; Rodger used his teeth. He could caress with his teeth, or bite. He would nip just hard enough to excite me, so I'd be hovering on the border between pain and ecstasy. In minutes I'd be burning like a furnace. Then he'd stoke me to white heat. The sensations went absolutely everywhere. Then for a few moments I'd be somewhere outside myself, sailing among the spheres of another universe. It was absolutely sublime. I couldn't get enough of him.

Rodger fascinated me. Not because he was physically attractive, although he was, and not because he was a superb lover, although he certainly was that. It was more the thrill of dealing with something dangerous. With Rodger you always felt on the edge, slightly out of control. I began to understand the buzz people got from keeping pets like pythons or leopards.

One way or another I'm afraid Rodger was just about the opposite of the stable, caring relationship Mummy and Daddy would have wanted for me, and that I could have had with Mike. But as I said before, I wasn't looking for a husband and a father; I wanted excitement. With Rodger I got it. In spades.

31

When I told Siobhan I was moving in with Rodger she was aghast.

"Suzy, darlin', are you sure you know what you're doing?"

"Yes, quite sure."

"You haven't fallen in love with this feller, or anything silly like that?"

"No, I don't think so. It's hard to explain. Look, I was in a rut, okay? It seemed to me that I'd already had all the excitement I was ever going to get out of life. All I could look forward to now was a boring marriage to a boring man, living in a boring house, bringing up two or three children, and maybe going back to a boring job at the bank."

"And what's so bad about that? Most people I know would settle for that. My old grandmother used to say if you had a man who didn't beat the bejezus out of you every Saturday night you could thank your stars."

"That was two generations ago, Siobhan. Things have changed, you know that. Women want more out of life now. I certainly do. I just knew something was missing but I couldn't put my finger on what it was. Then Rodger walked in. He's the most exciting person I've ever met; it makes my blood race just to be in the same room with him. It may not last—it probably won't—but if I let this go now I think I'll always be looking back and wondering what might have happened."

Siobhan shook her head dubiously. I knew she was genuinely concerned for me. I put my hand on her arm.

"Please don't worry," I said. "I'm not burning my bridges. I'll keep most of my stuff here and I'll carry on sharing the rent with you. I don't think Rodger is the type who wants a stable relationship, so sooner or later it will all be over and when that happens I'll come back. In the meantime, look at the upside: you'll have this whole place to yourself. You don't mind being on your own for a bit, do you?"

"No, that part of it doesn't bother me at all."

"And you'll have complete freedom—you'll be able to entertain boyfriends here and you'll never have to worry about what time I'm going to get home!"

Siobhan blushed. She's unlucky in that respect. Like some other redheads I've known, she has a creamy complexion and freckles and any emotion is immediately written all over her face. Right now her cheeks were crimson. Whereas I'm quite happy to succumb to my natural drives Siobhan always seems to be guilt-ridden about hers. It must be the result of her strict Catholic upbringing. I knew she'd had men in the flat but it was something we didn't talk about normally. We respected each other's privacy—that's why we got on so well. I hadn't meant to embarrass her. I was very fond of her.

She ran her tongue round her lips. "What about the other feller—Mike?" she asked.

"Yes, it's a shame Mike found out, but I guess it was only a matter of time. I know he was very hurt. I tried to let him down lightly but the damage was done."

"It's his flat, isn't it? What's he got to say about it?"

"He was very good about it. I mean, he's agreed to let me come and live with them and that can't have been easy for him."

"I don't know why he'd even contemplate such an arrangement. He should have chucked the pair of you out. He must be a real wimp."

"No, he's not! It happened rather suddenly, that's all, and it's left him feeling a bit helpless. I don't think he has much experience in dealing with people, least of all women. He's a really nice steady guy, though. You'd like him. Hey—maybe I should introduce you!"

"Thanks, but no thanks." She fixed me with her greeny-blue eyes. "You know what I'm thinking?"

"No, what?"

"I'm thinking he probably knows as well as you do that this Rodger thing isn't going to last. And when it all comes crashing down, he'll be around to pick up the pieces."

*

All the time I was staying at Mike's flat I had the feeling that they were up to something. I don't know what it was: an exchange of glances, a subdued conversation—I knew it wasn't just their research. To start with I thought it had something to do with me, but that didn't make any sense, so I put it down to my imagination.

I should have realized there was more to it when the bank's security people found all that money at Mr. Meredrew's house. I've got to admit I detested the man but I never wanted him dead. I knew I was involved in some way and I was feeling dreadfully guilty. What made it even worse was that he had a daughter in her teens. That set me imagining how I'd feel if Daddy committed suicide. Of course, she may not have been very fond of her father—it was hard to think of any youngster having feelings for someone as obsessional and demanding as Meredrew—but somehow that didn't make it any better. Mike took my mind off it with his play-acting. And, with or without the entertainment, it was a terrific dinner he put together that night. We finished up with ice-cream and I made some coffee.

Then all of a sudden everything changed. Mike was back to his normal self and saying, apparently in deadly earnest, "Now boys and girls. Who would like to be seriously rich?"

Rodger and I stared at him blankly.

He turned to me. "Suzy, how long till Lynsey gets her job back?"

"I... I hadn't thought..."

"Not long, is the answer. They can't do it immediately because it would be too embarrassing for them to admit they backed the wrong man. But they're not going to tribunal. Meredrew was under suspicion of embezzlement, so his judgment will be regarded as suspect, and that includes the way he dealt with Lynsey. She'll be back all right. They haven't given you a promotion yet, have they?"

"Well, no..."

"No, and they're not going to. They just expect you to take more responsibility for the same money. When she comes back she'll be the senior person again and you'll be back on the counters. Are you happy with that?"

"For God's sake, what are you saying, Mike?"

I was perplexed. I could see Rodger was too.

"I'm saying that you don't have to take this sort of shit any more. And neither does Rodge, and neither do I. Right now we have a window of opportunity. We have a chance to act, and if we don't grab it with both hands we'll be kicking ourselves for the rest of our dreary lives."

I looked at him uncomprehendingly.

Rodger said, "Maybe you should lay it out a bit for us, Mike."

"Look. We've already talked about the procedure for taking the money from the safe to the counters every morning. It's not just counters, though. There are two cash machines at that branch, in the outside wall where the customers can use them at any time."

"Mike!" I said. "You can't get at those ATMs!" I was reluctant to go into detail, but the ATMs are like safes, complete with combination locks, and the room behind them is equipped with infra-red and movement sensors. "Believe me, Mike, they're totally secure."

"All right, okay, okay. But people are drawing money out of those things all the time. It's a customer service, and you've got to provide it twenty-four hours a day, seven days a week, throughout the year. So if, for example, there's a bank-holiday weekend you've got to make sure they're stocked with enough money to see it through." He smiled engagingly at both of us. "There's a bank-holiday weekend coming up towards the end of this month."

I felt uncomfortable and I didn't say anything. To my amazement Mike rounded on me.

"Come on, Suzy. Don't be coy with me now. This is the future we're talking about: for you, for me, and for Rodge. So just tell me: am I on the right track, or am I not?"

I swallowed hard.

"Yes," I said. "You are."

32

Mike finished off his coffee. He'd never behaved as assertively as this before, certainly not towards me. I was quite shaken. It was like I was seeing him for the first time.

He put the mug down. His gaze had never left me but now it softened a little.

"Okay, good. Now that's a lot of money, and it has to be delivered to the branch, presumably by a security firm."

"Mike, I don't like this. If you or Rodger tangle with those people you're going to get hurt. Can't we…"

"We're not going to tangle with them. The point I'm making is: after that delivery there is going to be a large amount of money in the safe, enough to fill the machines for the bank-holiday and, for all I know, refill them the following week. All I want to know is, when is it going to be there, and how long is it going to stay there?"

Again I said nothing.

"Look, Suzy, there's a bank-holiday weekend coming up. You have to know when the delivery is going to be made, don't you? It's part of your working schedule."

"Yes," I said, weakly.

"Okay, so when's it to be?"

"Mike…."

"When?" he demanded.

"Thursday. Seven-thirty in the morning. Oh, Mike, I wish you hadn't started this."

I ran my hand through my hair and stole a desperate glance at Rodger. Why on earth hadn't he intervened? He looked at me, and for a moment I thought he was going to say something, but then he just looked back at Mike. I suppose he was curious to know what Mike had in mind. I didn't like the sound of it one bit, but Mike showed no sign of relenting. He seemed to be driven by a strange energy and he just kept up the pressure. I couldn't take it. I had a choice: either I rushed out of the room or I stayed there and answered his questions. Why I chose to stay, God only knows.

"All right. Now we're getting somewhere. So here come the heavy duty guys with the sticks and helmets. Who will open the street door to them?"

"We both will."

"Both?"

"Yes. Caroline's doing it with me. I have to be there to check the security man's pass."

"And then?"

"Then one of them brings in the first case. The others stand guard outside. Caroline locks the door behind him and stays there. I take him through to the secure area and open the safe."

"The money's packed in the case?"

"Not loose, no! It's in a thick polythene bag."

"Right, so he takes the bag out and puts it straight into the safe?"

"Not right away. I just check quickly that the contents of the bag tally with the delivery tag and then it goes into the safe."

"And then that's repeated with the other bags?"

"Yes. Two of the men take it in turns, so as one goes out

with an empty case the other one comes in with a full one. They want to get the whole thing over as quickly as possible."

"What do you mean 'as quickly as possible'? How long does it take?"

"Half an hour."

"Right. So let's say the delivery's finished. At this point the largest amount of cash that this branch ever handles is sitting in the safe in bags. Enough to keep the ATMs and the counters and the Friday payouts going for…how long? How often you get deliveries?"

"We're a busy branch; we used to get two a week. They're less frequent now. Deliveries were expensive and the bank decided to cut costs. Now they use a different firm with armoured trucks and a very high level of security, and they carry bigger amounts in the bags and make the drops less often. So after this delivery we're not scheduled to take another for two weeks."

"Two weeks?" He closed his eyes. I could almost see his mind working. He opened his eyes again. "There's got to be not far short of two million in there!"

"You're very smart, Mike. I think it will be about that. God, don't ever let on to anyone that I said so!"

"Of course not."

I felt a bit bad about passing on confidential information but in a way it didn't make any difference. Our procedures had been worked out in detail by the bank's security division in close consultation with the carriers and we followed them to the letter. These people were professionals. Mike was simply barking up the wrong tree; there was nothing he could do. All the same I felt a bit uneasy. He seemed to be following some line of reasoning that was hidden from me.

For a few moments nobody said anything. I was half

hoping it was over, but Mike picked up the thread again.

"Okay, the money's sitting there, in bags, at about eight a.m."

"Yes. And the safe door is locked," I added emphatically. "I do that as soon as I've seen Security off the premises."

"But it's got to go out to the ATMs and the counters. When does that happen?"

"That may not happen till midday. We have to bring in the staff to help with counting the notes before the money's distributed. But it's perfectly safe in there, Mike, I assure you."

"Tell me about that."

I actually laughed, just briefly. I couldn't believe I was having this conversation. Mike was waiting for an answer, his eyes drilling into me, but I was beginning to feel angry about being put on the spot like this. I adopted the patient tone of voice you might use for a troublesome child.

"It's a large wall safe with a combination lock and a key. It's set in concrete, okay? The door is steel, two inches thick. And it's in a secure area. Satisfied?"

Mike ran his tongue quickly around his lips. Then he smiled and said quietly: "Suzy, I know this is hard for you, but try to cooperate. You won't regret it, I promise you. Now, tell me about the secure area."

"What do you want to know?" I snapped, but my anger was subsiding. "Entry is controlled by key pad. There are infra-red and motion sensors, linked to the alarm system—"

"—which are switched off while you're in the area—" he interrupted.

"Well, yes, of course. And there's a steel shutter to the entire area too."

"Oh, really? Is that usual?"

"Actually I've never seen one before. The bank had it fitted as extra security around the time they went over to the bigger deliveries. They fitted a larger wall safe and the shutter at the same time. Maybe they'll bring them in at other branches too."

"And it's linked to the alarm?"

"Yes. Our security firm tests it when they check the alarm systems every six months. I've never seen it down at any other time. But if there's any alarm at all, anywhere in the building, it comes down automatically and seals off the secure area."

"What about closed circuit TV?"

I hesitated. "No... not in the secure area."

"You're sure of that?"

"Yes, quite sure—I just hadn't thought about it before, that's all. It's not really needed in there, you see. We don't have staff sitting around all day watching a monitor. If someone's in the secure area the sensors will pick up their movements or body heat and set the alarm off straight away. And if the police want mug shots, well, there's no way anyone could get as far as that without being caught on camera somewhere along the route. Mike, I don't know what you've got in mind but you might as well forget it. You're never going to..."

But just then I glanced at Rodger and the look on his face stopped me dead in my tracks. He was smiling, and there was a strange light in his eyes.

33

When I got back from work the following evening, Mike said: "Hi, Suzy. Rodge and I are having a little aperitif. Would you like to join us?"

I went and sat down in the kitchen with them. Mike busied himself at the counter and then slid a gin and tonic across the table to me. The ice clinked gently in my untouched glass. I wasn't being taken in by any of this. The interrogation had ended abruptly the previous evening and they'd said nothing more about it. But Mike's plan, whatever it was, clearly wasn't off the agenda. I'd known something was going on the moment I walked through the door.

"What are you two up to?" I said, looking from one to the other. "Come on, out with it."

Mike just smiled. It was Rodger who responded.

"Suzy, you know what we were talking about last night?"

He was trying to sound casual, I could hear it in his voice. I said nothing, just watched him through narrowed eyes.

"Well, we think it's time we did a little demonstration for you. Just to show you what we can do. It won't take long; maybe an hour all told. I think you'll find it very interesting. Is that okay?"

"You're up to something, aren't you?"

"Yes, we are. But we can't really discuss it unless you see our little demonstration first. Will you go along with us at least that far?"

"All right. What do I have to do?"

"Nothing. You just stay here. We have to go over to the lab."

"Are you coming straight back, then?"

"No, only when we've finished."

I laughed. "Some demonstration! I'm not going to see much if I'm over here and you're over there in the lab, am I?"

"Look, bear with us, all right? It takes a bit of understanding, this. I promise things will be clearer in an hour's time."

I shook my head. These two were playing silly games and they wanted me to join in. It really was too much at the end of a day's work.

Mike said, "Let's synchronize watches."

I sighed noisily. "My, my, we are being military about this, aren't we?"

I found two chunky wristwatches thrust under my nose. I couldn't very well ignore them. I adjusted my little bracelet watch so that the times coincided.

"Let's say twenty to seven," Mike said to Rodger. "That'll give us enough time to warm the equipment up." He turned to me. "At twenty to seven, Suzy, can you please stand in the doorway to the lounge, here? Just watch the lounge. That's all you have to do."

I must have looked totally mystified, which was understandable because I was.

"Suzy," Rodger said. "Promise you won't actually go into the lounge. Just stay in the doorway."

"Why? Oh, never mind. Okay. Whatever. I think you've gone stark raving bonkers, the pair of you."

And I stalked off to change my clothes.

*

I heard the front door close behind them. I couldn't be bothered to think about it any more. Once I'd changed into something more comfortable I settled down with a glossy, glancing at my watch from time to time. Six-thirty passed and I got involved in an interesting item on scuba diving on the Great Barrier Reef. That was something I'd always wanted to do. I thought I'd make some notes and then maybe I could cost it out and see how long it would take me to save up to do something like that. Caroline had been to the Maldives. She said the diving there was fantastic. Which would be better? I fancied Australia. It was further to go but then there'd be lots of other places I could visit while I was in the area…

I'd forgotten all about the time. I don't know what made me glance at my watch but when I did it said twenty to seven. I leapt up with a start, rushed over to the doorway and turned to face the lounge. As I did so, Rodger literally materialized in the middle of the room. A moment earlier the lounge had been empty and now there he was. I nearly jumped out of my skin. My knees buckled and I had to grab hold of the doorway just to keep from falling. Rodger stepped forward and took me by the arm, and helped me to the sofa. I was staring straight ahead, trembling with shock, heart banging, and breathing like I'd just run up six flights of stairs. When the immediate effects started to subside I wanted to cry but I couldn't. It took a long time for me to regain my composure. By the time I had, surprise had given way to anger.

"Rodger, you rotten b…," I compressed my lips to keep back the expletive. "You gave me the fright of my life. What made you want to play a trick like that on me?"

"It's no trick, Suzy."

"What do you mean, it's no trick?"

"I mean I can appear like this anywhere. I've invented a form of molecular transport, you know, the sort of thing you've seen in *Star Trek*?"

I was staring at him, transfixed. "But, how…?"

"Look, I have to get back to the lab. Mike and I will tidy up over there and then we'll come back and we can talk about it some more. Are you going to be all right?"

I swallowed hard. "Yes, I suppose so."

"Just one more thing. Can you get your handbag?"

I wasn't really thinking straight. I got up shakily and went and got my bag. When I came back I noticed he had a leather duffel bag and he was holding it open for me.

"That's good, put it in here. It's part of the demonstration. You'll get it back later. I want you to see that all this isn't just a trick."

I dropped it into the duffel bag and Rodger drew the closure tight. Then I thought, *Wait a minute, what am I doing? It's got my keys, my credit cards, my cheque book, my driving licence…*

It was too late. He stepped back and disappeared.

I reached out, trying to touch the empty air where he'd been only a moment before. Then I sat down with a thump. My head was in complete turmoil.

MIKE, SUZY AND RODGE

34

That morning Suzy had gone to work as usual. I hadn't pushed her for any more information; for the moment I had enough to go on with. What I needed now was to discuss the whole thing in more detail with Rodge. He hadn't stirred yet. I'd been sitting in the kitchen ever since Suzy went out, reading a newspaper, waiting for him to get up. Finally he made it into the land of the living and I tackled him while he was drinking his coffee.

"Can we talk about this job, now?"

"Sure, go ahead."

"Well, it's not as easy as it looks. If Suzy gets us the GPS coordinates for the secure area we can drop you right outside the safe. That part's not a problem. The problem is the sheer amount of money."

"How do you mean?" It seemed Rodge hadn't surfaced entirely.

"Well, for a start, that bag of yours isn't going to be big enough."

That woke him up.

"I'm not taking another bag and that's flat. I'm used to this one. It works for me. In any case, when I'm projected I only have half my normal strength—remember? If you give me a bigger bag and I fill it with paper money I won't be able to lift it."

"I thought you'd say that. Well then, we're going to have to make several trips."

"There won't be time. The security men finish the delivery at eight a.m. The girls come in to collect their tills at eight-thirty. We need to leave at least five minutes as a safety margin at each end. That gives us only twenty minutes."

"I know. Look, it's not impossible. The first question to ask is: how many trips? By the way, is the bag here or at the lab?"

"It's here. I brought it back here after the last job—the one we did on Friday at Suzy's bank."

"Okay. Let's use the money in the suitcase to see how much we can get into it at one time."

I went and got the suitcase. Most of the money we'd taken from the post offices and bank counters was still there—we'd been careful about spending too much because we didn't want to draw attention to ourselves. Rodge had taken out five thousand pounds to deposit in his bank account and the last fifteen thousand had never made it as far as the suitcase because we'd used it to stitch up Meredrew. Even so there was about a hundred and twenty thousand to work with. It hadn't been sorted very neatly. Some of it was still bundled and we started with that and sorted the rest as we went along. When we'd finished, the duffel bag was about half full.

"Looks like it'll take about two hundred and fifty thousand. That's only an estimate because we have no idea of the mix of denominations. I'm assuming there'll be a lot of tens and twenties though, so it won't be less than that."

Rodge hefted it. He grunted.

"It'll be a bit heavy when it's full."

"You won't have to lift the bloody thing while you're there. Leave it on the floor while you're loading it. You'll have no problem lifting it when you're back in the cage."

Rodge frowned. "Two hundred and fifty thousand on each trip," he said. "That means eight trips. In twenty minutes. Two-and-a-half minutes to fill the bag, return to the cage, empty the bag, bring up the power, and project out again… It can't be done."

"I think it can. Let's work through it step by step. Normally Suzy would see the security men off the premises and then go back and lock the safe. Only this time it's different. To the others she seems to be going through the usual routine but when she gets to the secure area she doesn't lock the safe. Instead she phones us on her mobile. That way we maximize the time available to us. If they go at eight sharp, and we've got our starting blocks on, we can have twenty-five minutes instead of twenty."

"That's better, but—just a minute. The police are bound to look at all the staff's mobile phone records. They'll suspect inside help the moment they realize there aren't any signs of a break-in. And when they check Suzy's they'll see that she made that call."

"Mmm. Okay, here's what we can do. I'll buy a cheap pay-as-you-go mobile phone. She only has to make one call on it. Just to make sure she doesn't misdial we'll program every button with my number. Then all she has to do is hold down one of the buttons and she comes through to me. That's my cue to project you. When you get there and start loading the money she bungs the phone in the bag as well, so you bring it back with you on the first trip. We can dispose of it later. As far as the cops are concerned, it never existed. They'll run their checks on the records for her usual mobile."

"Are there any calls to us on that one?"

"Not since she moved into the flat—there's been no need,

has there? There might be some before that, but they won't be incriminating. The cops are only going to be interested in calls made during the run-up to the job."

Roger nodded slowly.

"All right," he said. "I think that covers it. So we can have a full twenty-five minutes. Big deal. It's still only three minutes a trip."

"Hang on, you haven't heard it all. We use two duffel bags, not one."

Rodge opened his mouth to protest but I interrupted.

"Two bags exactly the same as that one. You take one on your first trip. You fill it and bring it back to the cage. I take the full bag from you and swap it for the empty one, and set up to project you again. While you're there I'm busy emptying the full bag so it's ready for the next trip; it all saves time. Then we just repeat the process. On the eighth trip you bring back the last bag. Job done."

That way we could probably cut thirty seconds off each trip, which would start to bring the whole thing within the realms of possibility. I thought he'd be pleased with the idea. He was nodding all right but his face was clouded and I had an inkling of what was running through his mind.

"It's a good plan, Mike," he said carefully. "The only thing is, it occurs to me that someone less scrupulous than yourself might get other ideas when they had seven bags of money, already totalling nearly two million pounds, in front of them. I mean, it might turn their heads. They might be tempted just to take the money at that point and leave me in resonance, if you see what I mean."

I looked at him, gave him a half-smile, and said in an indulgent tone of voice:

"Rodge. Don't be fucking silly."

"It's not an unreasonable point to make, is it, Mike? After all, I'm trusting you with my life, here."

"You've been doing that for weeks. What makes this job different? Look, it would be really smart for me to leave you for the cops to find, wouldn't it? So you could lead them straight back to me? Come on now, if we're going to do this properly we've got to work together. This kind of talk is going to get us nowhere."

He grimaced but it looked like he'd let it ride.

"Suppose someone comes in?" he asked. "That new manager, for example."

"You're going to have to sock him."

"Oh great! Have you forgotten I'm only punching half my weight?"

"I don't mean a right hook. You'll have to hit him over the head. Either come up behind him or, if he's facing you, threaten him with the gun, get him to turn round and then hit him with it."

"Sorry, I can't do that. I haven't got a clue how much force to use. I could just hurt him or I could kill him. I mean, I lost my rag with that woman who had a go at me, and I just hit her hard, but I've no idea whether she was stunned for a few seconds or out for hours. Anyway, Suzy wouldn't stand for any rough stuff. She likes that Welsh chap, and she's not going to go along with anything that ends up with him being badly hurt."

"Yeah, I think you're right. It'll have to be a stick-'em-up job, then. You're bigger and fitter than him, aren't you? He's not going to put up any resistance. Get him to lie down on his face and tie his hands and feet. And tie a pillow-case over his head so he can't see what's going on."

"We'll have to use a clean pillow-case, or forensic might

find something."

"Not clean, bloody brand new, I'm not taking any chances. I'll buy one. I'll also buy some rope and cut it into the right lengths to save time. You'll have to use latex gloves in case you leave fingerprints on the polythene bags. And you'll wear the balaclava, of course."

"Damn. I hate that balaclava. It's so bloody hot to work in. Maybe the manager won't come in."

"Maybe he won't, but we've still got to be prepared for it."

"I suppose you're right. Okay, let's see how we're doing for time. Suppose we use two bags, the way you said, and each trip lasts—how long?"

"Doing it like that? I'd say two-and-a-half minutes would be about enough."

"All right, eight trips, two-and-a-half minutes each—that's twenty minutes. Allow for one trip where someone like the Manager comes in and I've got to stop and tie them up—say another five minutes. Twenty-five minutes exactly. It's bloody tight, Mike."

"We're going to have to rehearse it. We can set the coordinates for this flat. The lounge is the biggest room, we'll project to that. We'll practise getting you here and back as smartly as we can. Then we can practise loading the duffel bag. See what we can get the time down to. If we can cut just a few seconds off each trip it'll mount up over eight trips. When we've got the basic operation really slick we'll practise dealing with interruptions at every different point. You can tie me up. We'll do the whole thing in perfect silence and time it with a stopwatch till it's perfect."

"And Suzy?"

"It'd be good if she could snaffle a half a dozen of those polythene money bags so we can work with the real thing.

There must be a few empty ones lying around; I don't suppose they just throw them away."

"No, I mean you're assuming that Suzy is on board. She's going to need a bit of persuading."

"Oh, I see. Rodge, I think the only thing for it is to do a demonstration for her. She's not going to be convinced by anything less. We've got nothing to lose. If she backs out she won't be able to tell anyone what happened; they'd think she'd gone crackers."

"You're right. Let's do it tonight. She can stay here while we go over to the lab. Then you can project me into the lounge."

"You can't do it just like that, Rodge, it'll give her the fright of her life! We have to prepare her in some way."

"I don't know. You saw what she was like last night. Right now, she's convinced it can't be done. We need to show her it can. Perhaps we do need to shock her a bit to change her mind. If we told her too much beforehand it would dilute the impact."

I thought about it and decided he was probably right. "Okay, we'll have to risk it. Let's clear the lounge and read the GPS coordinates for the middle."

We went into the lounge. Rodge turned the bed back into a sofa and we started shifting the furniture. Then he stopped and turned to me.

"You know, Mike, I ought to take something back with me as well. That way she'll see what's possible. It'll make the entire operation clearer."

"That's a good idea. You need something that'd be impossible to replicate. What about a notebook or something with her writing in it?"

He thought for a moment, then looked at me. "Her handbag," he said.

"Her handbag?"

"Yes. She'll recognize that, and she'll know straight away if the contents have been disturbed. But a handbag's good psychologically, too. Women get emotionally attached to their handbags; they grieve when they're parted from them. It'll raise her anxieties further if she loses touch with it. And then, when I give it back to her, she'll be correspondingly relieved, and that will increase her confidence in us. It's the sort of thing magicians do, you know, when they make objects disappear. They don't choose any old object; they choose something that's valuable to you, like your house keys."

"Very subtle. All right, that's agreed then. We'll set the whole thing up for her when she gets back from work. I just hope she has a strong constitution."

35

Inside the lab, Rodge's arm went up and I returned him to the cage. He opened the door and came out with the duffel bag. I looked at him expectantly.

"She's pretty shaken up, Mike."

"I was afraid that would happen. Did you try to explain it to her?"

"I just said it was a bit like the molecular transporter in *Star Trek*. I thought that would be easier for her to grasp, but I'm not sure she's taking anything in at the moment."

"Did you get her handbag?"

Rodge opened the duffel bag and showed me.

"Good. Well, let's pack up and go to her as quickly as we can."

When Rodge and I got back to the flat, Suzy was moving restlessly around. From the glass she was carrying I'd say she'd been working her way through a second gin and tonic, and a sizeable one at that. She stopped and glared at us.

"There you are," she said. "Nice of you to use the front door for a change. I hope you've finished with your little games for the evening."

Rodge said, "I'm really sorry, Suzy. We couldn't think of any other way of doing it. Are you all right now?"

"Oh, I suppose so. God, I don't know what gave me a bigger turn: you appearing in the middle of the room or the expression on your face just before you disappeared."

She was obviously talking about the moment when Rodge transferred his awareness back into the cage. Rodge seemed intrigued.

"What expression?" he asked.

"Oh, it was like a vacant stare. All the life went out of your face. You looked like a dead person standing up. Gave me the shivers."

She shuddered, then peered at him, as if half expecting to see the same expression again. Rodge, however, was busy opening the leather duffel bag. He reached in, came out with her handbag, and handed it to her. She opened it quickly and, of course, found the contents undisturbed. She was visibly relieved.

"How did you manage it?" she asked him wonderingly.

"It's a bit complicated to explain, Suzy. The technicalities needn't really concern us, though. The fact is I can. I've shown you I can. What more can I say?"

Her big brown eyes swept from one of us to the other. She'd obviously been doing some frantic thinking while we'd been finishing off in the lab.

"That's how you did it, isn't it? That's how you stole the money from the tills in my Bank and left them locked."

"I told you I could guarantee," I said, a little truculently.

"And that's how you planted the money on poor Mr. Meredrew."

Rodge reacted quickly to that.

"Poor? The man was a reptile, Suzy!" he said. "Don't waste your sympathy on him. In any case we only meant to get him into hot water. Things got a bit out of hand, that's all."

She turned and went back into the lounge. Rodge and I followed, moved the armchairs and the coffee table back into their usual positions, and we all sat down. Suzy looked at Rodge.

"And now you want to rob a bank."

"Not quite," he said. "I want *us* to rob a bank. Suzy, we're not talking about till drawers here. We're talking about two million pounds in used, untraceable notes. We'll be rich. We'll be able to go anywhere in the world. It'll be like winning the lottery, except that we can make it happen. And no one will ever know how it was done."

"So do it. You don't need me."

"Yes we do. Mike, you explain."

"Look, Suzy," I said. "You've seen how Rodge can transport himself with this invention of his. He can go through walls, trees, everything. But we have to set the destination very accurately. We do that by taking a sort of reading in the place where he's going to land. It's very simple: just a device like a mobile phone. All you do is press a few buttons. That's how you can help us. We'll show you how to use it to take a reading in the secure area. Then Rodge will be able to land right outside the safe."

"But the safe's locked…"

I spoke with gentle emphasis. "Not this time. That's the other way you can help us. You 'forget' to lock it straight after the delivery's been completed. You can lock it later after Rodge has got all the money out."

"Oh, wonderful. Look, Mike, good employees don't forget things like that, and I'm a good employee. And just suppose for the moment that I still have time to go back and lock the safe after you. What then? Off I go, trying to look nonchalant, and I get a cup of coffee or occupy myself with something else. The next thing that happens is the girls come looking for me to open up the safe because they need to take their tills to the counters. So I open up and wow, am I surprised when we look inside and see that all the money's gone! Do you really think anyone is going to believe I had nothing to do with it? I'm the one who knows how to operate the safe. It's my job to lock it after the delivery. My God, they'll probably reckon I let the robbers in and out of the door myself."

Rodge said, "She's got a point, Mike."

"Okay, okay, let's think this through. Look, Suzy, we can do it like this. You come to the secure area as usual, as if you're going to lock the safe. You phone us when you get there; that way we know the coast is clear. As soon as Rodge arrives he ties you up. When the girls come in for their tills they'll find you tied up on the floor. It'll look like a robbery. That way you won't fall under suspicion yourself."

She grimaced slightly and thought about this for a moment. "And what happens when I don't turn up for work the next day? They're still going to put two and two together, aren't they?"

I was watching her carefully. She seemed to be taking a different tack, not objecting to the plan in principle but showing us it was unworkable. That was a good sign. As for the point she was making, I'd already given that some thought.

"After the raid they're bound to want to take you to hospital to get you checked over. They'll release you once they've established there aren't any actual physical injuries. You go back to your own flat and stay there. Over the next couple of days you tell your girlfriend you're suffering from post-traumatic stress. 'It was all so ghastly and it keeps coming back to me in flashbacks and nightmares. I haven't slept a wink since it happened'—you know the sort of thing. Your colleagues at the bank are sure to phone to find out how you are. You get her to take the calls and make sure she feeds it all back to them. You let a couple more days go by, then you phone the manager—what's-his-name?—Hughes. You tell him just the thought of coming back to the place where it all happened sets your nerves screaming. Right now you don't know how long it will last. It could go on for years. You think it's only fair to resign from your position at the bank. You can't imagine ever wanting to go back into banking but maybe when you're feeling better you'll try some other career. He probably won't try to talk you out of it. He'll be very sorry to lose you, of course, but on the other hand it will be a relief, because he'll be able to fill the vacancy. Do it properly, though, it'll look suspicious if you don't. Get your P45, ask about transferable pension rights, get him to write you a letter of recommendation. It should only take a week or two at most. Then you can join us."

She smiled sweetly at us. "Always assuming that you haven't just taken the money by then and done a runner."

We both shook our heads.

Rodge said, "Suzy, there's no need for that. You surely can't believe I'd want to leave without you! We'll be here at the flat. We'll be in no hurry; there's absolutely no way they can trace us or connect us to the robbery. All the same it's probably best if you don't actually come round here, just in case someone is watching you. We'll arrange to meet you somewhere."

"And how are you going to get the money out of there?" she demanded. "You're not talking about a handbag, now, Rodger. You're talking about—what?—forty bags of money."

"I won't be doing it in one go, Suzy. I'm going to make eight trips."

"Eight trips? That's five bags a trip. It's still a lot. What are you going to put it in?"

"The duffel bag. The one you saw before."

She gave a short laugh. "Never."

"What do you mean?"

"Those polythene bags are far too bulky. You'll never get five in that thing."

I hadn't thought of that. When we'd tried the duffel bag to see how much it would hold we'd done it with loose bundles of money. I glanced at Rodge. I could see that his mind was working furiously too. For a while we were both silent.

"There's nothing else for it," I said to him eventually. "We're going to have to open the money bags and transfer the cash to your duffel bag. Five on every trip."

Rodge sighed and shook his head.

"That's going to take time, Mike, and time is what we haven't got," he said. "We've just been talking about tying Suzy up. That's going to add another two or three minutes if you want me to make a convincing job of it. We're running too close to the wire. Unless…"

36

Mike and Rodger met each other's eyes. Then their heads turned and they were both looking at me.

"Oh no," I said. "What are you cooking up now, the pair of you?"

Mike pointed a finger.

"Slight change of plan, Suzy. Rodge doesn't tie you up as soon as he gets there. He ties you up *right at the end*. That way you can help him. Each time he arrives you can have five bags already out of the safe and opened so everything's prepared. He holds the duffel open and you tip the money in. We work as a team. It would speed things up no end."

"Oh, you've got me properly involved now, haven't you? And what will you be doing in the meantime?"

"Well, I'll be back in the lab operating the, er, transporter. And I'll have an identical duffel bag with me. Each time Rodge comes back with a full bag, I'll swap it for an empty one. It shaves more seconds off every run. I'll be emptying it while you two are filling the next one."

"And suppose someone comes into the secure area?"

Rodger said, "In the middle of everything, you mean?"

"Yes, that's exactly what I mean. In the middle of everything."

"Who's likely to do that?"

"Well, Caroline will be around, for a start, won't she?"

"You're senior to her, aren't you? Couldn't you give her something to do?"

I thought for a moment.

"I suppose I could ask her to do a book-keeping job and get her to sit down with it at the enquiries desk. She can keep an eye on the front door from there. I could tell her to look out for Mr. Hughes. He comes in early sometimes if there's a big delivery—he feels it's a lot of responsibility for us to carry. That way she wouldn't be walking in on us, and afterwards she could tell everyone that nobody came in or out by the front door."

Rodger said, "Brilliant!" and Mike was nodding vigorously.

I felt the heat in my face; it was so unusual to get praise from Rodger. I suppose they were pleased that I'd started to come up with solutions as well as problems. I tried to pass it off with a shrug.

"Well, it may not work. She might still come back to ask me something. And Mr. Hughes could actually turn up. What if he walks in?"

"We'll pretend you're acting under duress," Rodger said. "That won't be hard. I'll be carrying a gun."

He must have seen the alarm on my face.

"Don't worry, it's not a real gun! But if he comes in I'll point it back and forth between you so it looks like you're under threat as well. That way you're not compromised. Then I'll have to tie him up and put a pillow case over his head so he can't see what's going on. We'll have to work in total silence, too, so he doesn't hear anything either."

I considered this carefully.

"Just a minute. You won't be there all the time. Suppose someone comes in when you're not there? I could be standing there ankle deep in empty money bags with the safe wide open and no one in sight. I'm going to look very good then, aren't I?"

"We can't afford for that to happen," Rodger said.

"You're damned right we can't."

Mike chewed his lip thoughtfully. "It's pretty unlikely." His comment was directed more to Rodger than to me. "I mean you'll only be gone for about a minute each time, won't you, Rodge?"

"She's right, though, Mike, we've got to be prepared for it."

"Okay," Mike said. "How about this? As soon as she hears the door open she throws herself on the floor. Says she was knocked down by a robber."

"So where is he, this robber?" I asked.

"He was disturbed so he ran off."

Rodger said, "And at that moment I materialize in the room…"

"No, no, that's no good." Mike ran his hands through his hair. "I know. When they pick her up she does a fainting swan act. It's fair enough. She's been shocked. She can't breathe, she must have air. So they take her outside. If she makes a lot of fuss they'll all be focused on her. Anyway as soon as you arrive you'll see what's happened and you can signal to come back. We'll have to call it a day then."

"Someone may activate the alarm," Rodger said.

"That would be better still, wouldn't it? The alarm brings the shutter down and then they have to stay outside. They'll see even less." Mike paused; he seemed to have had another thought. "Suzy, that keypad thing you use to enter the secure area. When it's operated, does it make any noise?"

"Yes. The keys go bip, bip and when the right combination is entered it buzzes and then the lock releases. Why?"

"Well, that's very handy. It'll give us a bit of warning that someone's coming in. You'll have to practise being fast on the draw, Rodge. If the buzzer goes you've got to have the gun in your hand before they see you."

"It's okay. I'll be using the holster. I'm not wearing a jacket so I can get at it easily."

We fell silent.

I was glad to have a few minutes to collect my thoughts. It was beginning to dawn on me that what Mike and Rodger were planning was actually feasible. They'd scared the daylights out of me with their little demonstration but I could see the reason for it now. I'd never have believed them if they'd tried to convince me in some other way. Transport through walls! The possibilities that opened up! If we planned the operation carefully, so that we knew how to deal with every contingency, what could go wrong? No one would have a clue how it was done, and no one would imagine I'd been involved!

I didn't feel too badly about the bank. An organization of that size wouldn't lose any sleep over a mere two million pounds but it was a heck of a lot of money to me. Even split three ways it meant nearly seven hundred thousand apiece—more than I could save in a lifetime. I'd been thinking of getting out of this job anyway and I was dying to see more of the world. This could be my ticket.

37

When I looked up, Mike was staring into the carpet, frowning. Rodger said to him: "What's the matter, Mike?"

"I'm still worried about the timing. If you have to tie up both Suzy and the manager it's going to take eight minutes out of the twenty-five. That leaves seventeen minutes, and you have to do eight trips in that time. That's about two minutes a trip."

"That's going some," Rodger said. "Even with Suzy helping me at the bank end I'm not sure we could get it down to that."

"We'll just have to practise," Mike said. "We've got about three weeks; that ought to be enough. We'll rehearse every move. That includes you, Suzy. You'll have to practise with us."

"How?"

"Well, the way I see it, each trip is made up of two parts and we have to work on both of them. One part is what happens in the lab. I have to transport Rodge to the secure area, return him to the lab, take the full duffel bag and swap it for an empty one. The other part is loading the money into the duffel bag while he's in the secure area. You'll have to practise that bit with Rodge. He'll stand here as if I transported him and you'll have a bag of money ready…"

"Oh, and precisely where am I going to get a bag of money from?"

"Suzy," Rodger said quietly. "You're forgetting. That business with Meredrew—that didn't come out of the blue. It had to take place on a background of other robberies. That's what supposedly gave Meredrew the cover for stealing from his own bank. To make it convincing we had to raid a few other bank counters before we hit yours."

For the moment I'd forgotten all about that string of robberies; the shock of Rodger appearing in the lounge must have put it out of my mind. Now I could see it; the whole set-up. And then I remembered something else, and my stomach lurched.

"Rodger, a bank teller was badly injured in one of those raids…"

He waved a hand dismissively. "The Press exaggerated the whole thing wildly. She attacked me and I sloshed her, that's all. It was pure self-defence."

I looked at him, wondering whether I could believe that. Rodger wasn't capable of beating a girl unconscious, was he? I had an uncomfortable feeling that he was.

"Anyway," Mike continued, "you'll help him transfer the money to the duffel bag and I'll time it. We'll keep on rehearsing until we're fast enough."

"So when are you going to do all this? I have a day job, in case you hadn't noticed."

"The transport part is something Rodge and I can work on during the day—we can go to and from the lounge, like we did earlier this evening. Shifting the money from the bags to the duffel is something you'll have to do with us in the evenings. It's only for a few weeks. You'll see; it'll be worth it in the end."

I grimaced. In my mind, though, it was starting to come together. I take five bags of money out of the safe, open them, empty them into the duffel bag. While Rodger is transporting the money back, I'm opening five more. He returns with an empty bag. We repeat that eight times…"

"What about the money?" I asked. "Where are you going to keep all that money?"

Rodger said, "We can't leave it at the lab. I sort of assumed we'd bring it here. What do you think, Mike?"

"Well, we can't just walk out of the Department carrying a large suitcase—that would be asking for trouble. I was thinking we could transport it here. We could reset the coordinates for the lounge and take the money over in eight trips—a sort of reverse of what we'd done at the bank. We wouldn't have Suzy to help us, but that wouldn't matter. There wouldn't be a deadline. We could take our time."

Rodger shook his head. "I'm not happy about that. We're making eight trips in seventeen minutes. That equipment is going to start to get pretty hot. Some of it may go off tune. It's dangerous enough as it is without having to do a repeat performance."

"Take your point. Okay, how about I bring in a couple of large sports bags, one each, different makes? We can put the money in those and cover it up with a towel, just in case someone wants to take a peek inside. It's very unlikely anyone would stop us, though. I'll buy a couple of cheap squash rackets and racket covers and we can walk out around lunchtime carrying those and the bags as if we were going off to have a game."

"That's good. We just walk out and back to the flat. I like it."

They were both silent for a moment. Then Rodger said:

"You know, Mike, before we finally leave the lab we'll have to spend an hour or so disconnecting the equipment.

That way nobody will be able to reconstruct what we used it for. This will be the last job and we won't be going back there."

Mike looked surprised.

"Why does it have to be the last job? There won't be anything to associate us with it."

"Yes, there will: Suzy. Once she's cut her ties with the bank, she'll be joining us. We can't keep that quiet for ever. So long as she's around there's a chance that someone will start to put two and two together. Especially if we're stupid enough to start spending the money. No, what we have to do is lie low for a couple of weeks while Suzy goes through that post-traumatic stress routine of yours. Then she joins us and we leave the country pronto."

I started to shake my head. Rodger raised his eyebrows.

"What's the matter, Suzy?"

"It's getting out of hand, that's what. Now you're talking about going abroad as well. Total upheaval. I don't know, I'm beginning to wonder if it's worth it. Two million isn't all that much divided three ways."

"Hang on," Mike said. "Who said anything about a three-way split?"

I rounded on him. "Why, what did you have in mind?"

"Well," he said. "Rodge and I have an arrangement. Fifty-fifty, we agreed. You two are an item, so I figured you'd be sharing with him."

"What, twenty-five percent? No way! You can't do this without me and I'm taking a terrible risk getting involved at all. We split three ways or nothing."

I could see they were both taken aback. I was a little surprised myself. It seemed like only a few minutes ago I was thinking I'd be insane to get involved in this caper, and now here I was, ready to stand my ground about dividing the spoils!

"Be reasonable, Suzy," Mike said. "I'm not saying you aren't important to the project, and Rodge invented the technology that makes it possible, but the idea and the whole plan was mine. If we split three ways, you guys are going away with twice as much as me."

It went back and forth in this vein for quite a while. Then Rodger joined in. Finally we reluctantly agreed on a compromise. Mike would get forty percent, and Rodger and I would split the remaining sixty percent between us. It wasn't quite as much as I wanted, but it was better than twenty-five percent.

The atmosphere was still a bit charged, so it seemed a good idea to leave it there for the moment. We had a quick snack and went to bed. I said as little as possible—to either of them.

38

It's wonderful how a double bed can resolve disagreements. I'd been asleep for a while when I awoke to feel Rodger's foot touching my leg. I rolled over and felt the heat of his body through my nightdress. Before long we were making love as urgently as ever. Afterwards he put his arm round me and I nestled up close. My fingertips trailed down his chest and up again. I was thinking.

"Rodger?"

"Yes?"

"You wouldn't leave me behind, would you? You know, if everything goes well and you get the money, you wouldn't take it and leave me behind, would you?"

"Of course not. If nothing else it wouldn't be very clever for me to abandon you. You might suddenly remember something that led the police straight to my door."

I sat up slightly.

"That's a pretty negative thing to say. Don't you have any feelings for me at all?"

"Of course I do. But feelings are one thing and actions are another. I was just being practical."

I mulled that over for a bit.

"I can be practical too," I said. "I can be very useful to you. Two million pounds is a lot of money and it'll attract attention if you're not careful how you deal with it. But I know ways we could spread the money out in small parcels and get it converted into US dollars."

"Really?"

"Of course. What am I in the banking business for?"

We fell silent. Finally I asked: "What do you think of the plan?"

"I think it's good. Why?"

"I'll be taking a terrible risk. Mike doesn't seem to appreciate that."

"He's put a lot of thought into it. I suppose he feels he's covered most of the angles."

"I don't see why he should get more than me, or you for that matter. You're the brains behind the whole thing. He once said that he was just a hack technician. He told me that himself."

"That's true. But this thing was his idea."

"You can't see it, can you?" I whispered. "He's using you. Whose technology is it? Yours. Who goes in and takes all the risks? You. Mike's back in the lab. He's not taking any risks. But you're letting him walk out with the lion's share."

"What are you saying?"

"Mike's a single guy, Rodger. What does he need such a lot of money for? You know, if we're starting a new life together somewhere abroad we're going to need a lot more than him."

"How much more?"

"A lot more."

"I see. Go on."

"Well, when you bring the money back here to the flat you were planning to sit tight for a bit, weren't you? You said you would. Just while I extricate myself from the bank."

"Yes, that's right."

"Well, you'll have your usual routine. You know, like you

have now. Going shopping, going to the launderette."

"Yes."

"Come on, Rodger. Do I have to spell it out? What I'm saying is that he won't be able to keep an eye on you the whole time. You know, you might have the opportunity to—"

"—take all the money and run?"

"Well, maybe not all. You could leave him a hundred thousand."

He let out a soft little laugh.

I frowned. "What's funny?"

"Nothing." And then he said, "What makes you think Mike isn't planning to work the same trick on me? He could, you know. And then you and I would come out of all this without a penny."

That thought hadn't occurred to me. I was genuinely alarmed.

"You think he would? Oh God. Well, you'll just have to get in first."

"Relax, Suzy. I think you're underestimating Mike. He's very cute, you know. I bet he's already anticipated that someone might have a mental aberration at the sight of all that money. He's probably cooked up some plan for us to split the takings and put it in left luggage lockers, or something like that, so that none of us has access to any more than their own share. He's not brilliant, but he's sure as hell not stupid either. Let's just play it by ear. We haven't got to that stage yet, not by a long chalk. We're going to have to put in a lot of preparation—all three of us. When we've got the money... well, then we'll see. Come on now, let's get some sleep."

*

Rodger and Mike showed me how to use the GPS receiver and made me take readings all round the flat until they were sure I knew how to operate it. It went with me to the bank the next day. That evening I gave them the coordinates for the secure area. We'd made a start.

The following day I took a handbag to work that was a bit larger than the one I usually carry. When I returned to the flat in the evening Mike and Rodger watched me take out five of the thick polythene money bags for us to practise with. Mike was ecstatic. We did a trial run then and there. There wasn't enough money in the suitcase to fill all five bags so he'd bought a few reams of plain paper, cut them up with a craft knife and used paper bands to make them into bundles. They handled like banknotes, or near enough for our purposes.

Mike set his stopwatch going and Rodger and I started transferring the money to his duffel bag. It was a disaster. He was trying to help and we kept getting in each other's way, and then the duffel bag wouldn't stay open and there was money all over the floor. I got a fit of the giggles but Mike wasn't a bit amused.

"This is hopeless," he said, throwing up his hands. "You took nearly two minutes for that alone. We can't faff around like this; we've got to get our act together. Rodge: don't try and help her. You just concentrate on keeping that duffel bag of yours wide open. Suzy: have all the money bags open and place them in a line close to the duffel. You may have to take out the first few bundles by hand; then see if you can tip the rest in without spilling it everywhere."

We emptied the money and the paper bundles onto the carpet, sorted it into the five poly bags and started all over again. We managed it more tidily the next time, but it still wasn't quick enough so we did it again. And again. This sort of thing became the pattern for the days that followed.

I had to go to work, of course; it might have looked suspicious if I'd taken time off. The two chaps spent the time at the lab, seeing how quickly they could transport Rodger to the flat and back. In the evenings I'd get home and the three of us would practise transferring the money to the duffel bag. It wasn't ideal from my point of view because I'd already had a busy day at work and I was tired before we even started.

When we'd got that running fairly smoothly we practised dealing with interruptions. We'd start to transfer the money and then Mike would walk in without warning and Rodger would have to go through the routine of waving the toy gun at him and then tying him up with a pillowcase over his head. And all the time that wretched stopwatch would be running.

After a week of this I was exhausted. Rodger was, too. Even Mike was flagging, although he still drove us like a demon. When we were done with rehearsing for the evening we'd be ready for something to eat. It was too late to start cooking, and we didn't want to risk being seen together at a restaurant or fast-food place, so one of us would go out for a take-away. We got pretty sick of take-aways. Our spirits were low and even when we weren't rehearsing we were constantly snapping at each other. I was beginning to wish we'd never started this business.

The following week we started to put the separate parts together. We did it all in the lounge, with Mike miming the moves he'd normally be making in the lab. It seemed awfully complicated but Mike and Rodger were quite serious about simulating it properly. They placed cushions to mark the corners of something they called "the cage" and Mike would pretend to twiddle knobs and he'd spread his fingers to push something forward and flick imaginary switches. I hadn't a clue what he was up to but Rodger seemed quite satisfied. Then Mike would stab at something with his right forefinger while he brought the other hand down in a signal; I suppose that was the moment he activated the transporter. Rodger would open the duffel bag, I'd transfer the money, he'd close the bag and lift his arm, and Mike would do some more twiddling. Then Mike would run round the cushions, open a make-believe door, swap the full duffel bag for an empty one and click the stopwatch. We got the whole sequence down to about two-and-a-half minutes.

After that we had a go at doing it properly. We couldn't start until I got back from work and that meant Mike and Rodger had to stay on late at the lab; there was a slight risk of attracting attention to themselves but it couldn't be helped. Mike transported Rodger to the lounge; I helped him transfer the money to the duffel bag and Mike returned him to the lab. The only detail missing was that Rodger didn't actually take the duffel bag with him; as soon as he'd gone I had to empty it and sort the money into the poly bags so that we could do it all over again. The curious thing was, I was so focused on transferring the money as quickly as possible I hardly paid any attention to the fact that Rodger was now materializing next to me in the lounge. I simply took it for granted, even though it had given me such a dreadful shock the first time he did it.

I lost count of the number of repeat runs we did. Each time Rodger appeared he'd tell me what Mike's stopwatch had given us for the last trip. I barely registered it—by now I was going through the motions like an automaton. I remembered hearing him say two minutes thirty-five seconds earlier on, and at some stage it had come down to two minutes seventeen seconds. As far as I was concerned we'd reached the limit: there was no way I could do it any faster. Then it seems that one of them had an idea for shortening the routine for transporting Rodger; it knocked about fifteen seconds off each trip. When Rodger arrived for the final time he said, "Two minutes, three seconds, Suzy. This next run will be the last tonight."

As soon as he'd gone I pushed back my hair and flopped into an armchair. I was still there when I heard them come through the front door.

"Well done, people," Mike said as he came into the lounge. "Two minutes flat for the last run. On target at last. If we can keep that up for another week we're going to be rich."

I looked at him. "Mike, I've had it. I need a break."

"You've worked very hard, Suzy. Don't worry, I'll go out for the take-away. You'll feel better when you've had something to eat."

"You're not listening, Mike. I need a proper break. Tomorrow's Friday. I've decided to go down to Kent and spend a long weekend with my Mum and Dad."

There was a shocked silence. Mike was the first to react.

"For God's sake, Suzy! Of all times to want to go and visit your parents!"

"They're my parents, not yours, Mike. God only knows when I'll see them again. I have a duty towards them."

"Suzy," Rodger pleaded. "You're jeopardizing the whole thing. We've worked so hard for this. All we have to do is hold it together for a bit longer…"

"This is ridiculous! Will you two stop talking as if I'm letting you down? I told you, I need a break. What are you worrying about? We're on target."

"Correction," Mike said. "We've been on target once. That's not good enough. We've got to be able to do it consistently. A few seconds here and there may not seem to matter to you but it mounts up over eight trips."

"Look, I'm going and that's final. If you two don't like it you can jolly well do this little caper on your own."

The air had turned to jelly. Finally Rodger sighed.

"Maybe she's right, Mike. Maybe it would do us all good to get out of each other's company for a bit."

Mike looked like he was going to come out with something but then his shoulders slumped.

"All right, I give up. Have it your own way. I just hope we can get back up to speed by next Thursday, that's all."

39

The following morning I went into the bank as usual. I saw Mr. Hughes as soon as he was free.

"I do have some leave due, Mr. Hughes," I said. "I was wondering if you could possibly manage without me until Tuesday."

He was a bit taken aback.

"It's a bit sudden, this, isn't it, Susan?"

"I know, I'm terribly sorry. My mother's just recovering from the flu, you see, and now my father's got it and I said I'd go down and help out."

"Ah, well I suppose you better had, then. Can you make sure anything urgent is covered before you go?"

"Of course I will."

"I hope they'll be feeling better soon."

"Thank you very much."

So far as I know they're in rude health but I thought it would help. He's a dear man.

As I was about to leave the office he called out:

"Oh, and Susan—you know there's a secure delivery coming Thursday morning, don't you?"

"Yes, I do know. Thank you, Mr. Hughes."

As if I could forget.

I left at lunchtime and went back to my own flat. Siobhan wasn't going anywhere at the weekend and she'd agreed to lend me her little Renault to drive down to Kent. I crossed the River at Putney Bridge and took the South Circular. It was terribly congested all the way—I suppose there was a lot of traffic going out of town for the weekend. In spite of that, the journey seemed to pass quickly. Most of the time my mind was elsewhere; I was thinking about what was going to happen after the job.

Could I hold on to Rodger? It shouldn't be too hard. He was really into me by now—and not just in a crude sense. I was hoping he'd given some thought to the idea I'd put into his head. He was so much cleverer than Mike; surely he could find a way of outsmarting him? Then we'd have two million between us. Two million good reasons to stay together.

Would our relationship ever go deeper? It wouldn't be hard to love him, not when the physical thing was so strong. It would be easier if, just occasionally, he could show me a little affection. He was very cold that way. Probably he grew up in one of those aristocratic households where the son calls the father "Sir", and the mother's busy trying to reclaim her life after the minor aberration of having had children. I supposed it would take time.

Mike would be sore, of course, but it would pass. He wouldn't be able to blow the whistle on us without revealing his own part in the operation; he'd just have to keep quiet. And we'd cover our tracks carefully so he couldn't follow us.

If we took Mike's share as well, there wouldn't be time for all that post-traumatic stress disorder nonsense with the Bank; we'd have to skip the country pronto. Two million was a lot of cash to carry in suitcases, though. It would be best to go by sea. Security wouldn't be so tight that way either. We could get one of those sea-going trunks, pack the money in the bottom, and put clothes and stuff on the top. Cruise somewhere—what a lovely thought! There probably wouldn't be a schedule that fitted us exactly but we could always get a ferry over to Ireland or France and wait for the cruise ship there.

We could sail around the world and then settle somewhere nice. I fancied a place where it wouldn't cost too much to have servants. Southern California or Texas, perhaps. They get a lot of illegal immigrants there, crossing the border from Mexico; they'd work for next to nothing. I could have a cook and a gardener and someone to do the shopping and clean the house. I've got a little Spanish, but they'd have to learn English anyway...

I was feeling better already.

*

Daddy was working in the garden. He waved and came over to me but before he had a chance to say anything Mummy came out of the house in full sail, wearing a purple and green kaftan.

"Susan, darling!" She enveloped me.

"Hello, Mummy," I said weakly, as I surfaced.

"Let me look at you, dear," she said. She held me at arm's length and inspected me carefully from top to bottom before delivering the verdict. "My, my, you're looking well!"

She sounded surprised. So was I. It made quite a change from "You're looking a little peaky, dear. Are you eating properly?"

"Isn't she looking marvellous, Neville? Look at the roses in those cheeks! What have you been doing, darling? You're not in love, are you? Oh, you wouldn't tell me even if you were."

"Now, Mummy, don't be silly."

"Isobel and Geoffrey are coming over later for a coffee.

That'll be nice, dear, won't it? They haven't seen you for ages."

"Lovely."

Actually it would be seriously dull. Isobel and Geoffrey were old friends of the family. They'd all be talking ten to the dozen amongst themselves and my role would be to stay in the background with a fixed smile on my face, pretending to enjoy the company.

"And then tomorrow I thought we could go shopping together."

"They do have shops in London, Mummy."

"I know, dear, but we don't often get a chance to go shopping together. A mother should do that sort of thing with her daughter once in a while, now, shouldn't she?"

When it was a matter of what a mother's responsibilities were, there was no arguing with her. I knew perfectly well what would happen, though. She would do her best to influence what I bought, and that would be really annoying because I know what I like. And then she'd insist on making me a present of something that didn't suit me at all, and afterwards I'd have to chuck it or give it to Nadine.

Sometimes I felt I had nothing in common with my parents any more except my DNA. God knows why I still felt attached to them, but I did. I just wished Mummy would wake up to the fact that I'm not a little girl any more and stop trying to make all my decisions for me. Maybe it was just as well that I'd be leaving the country; it was the only way I'd ever really be free to do my own thing. I didn't want them to fret, though. I'd have to think of some way of letting them know I was safe without giving the game away.

"There's a new family moved into Number 24, Susan. They have a son about your age. He's very handsome."

Mummy gave me a significant look.

Oh yes? Is he a six-foot Greek god with a brain like Einstein's and the bedroom talents of Casanova? Otherwise it'd be a bit of a comedown, you see.

"I'm sure it would be lovely to meet him, Mummy, but there won't be much time for that. I have to go back Monday lunchtime. I've got work Tuesday morning, and I haven't done my washing or cleaned the flat yet."

She looked crestfallen. "Oh, I thought you could stay a while longer this time, Susan dear! It's been so long. Do you really have to rush away?"

"'Fraid so. It was really decent of the Manager to give me this long weekend. There's a lot to do at the moment."

Well wasn't that the truth! What would you say, Mummy, if you knew that your sweet little daughter was mixed up in a two-million-pound bank robbery? It might come as something of a shock, I imagine.

Daddy managed to get a word in, for the first time. "Now, Maureen, the girl's only just got out of the car and you're already making her head spin with arrangements. Let her get unpacked and settled in, there's a love."

"Oh, yes, I was forgetting! Neville, give her a hand with the luggage, would you…?"

"I can manage, Mummy."

"Nonsense! Neville? Right, off you go dear! And then you can show me what you're going to wear tonight. I know it's only coffee, but they are our friends and we want to give them the right impression, don't we?"

40

In retrospect Mike and I probably did over-react when Suzy said she was going to visit her parents. All the same I don't think we were being unreasonable. When you've got an operation running smoothly, as we more or less had, the last thing you want is a major interruption. And Mike and I had worked very hard in the lab, shaving seconds off the time needed to make each projection. We found that if Mike started to recharge the capacitor bank while I was still in resonance he could be ready to make the next projection almost as soon as he'd taken the full duffel bag and swapped it for the empty one. It reduced the turnaround by a full fifteen seconds and we clocked two minutes for the first time. At last, with less than a week to go before we hit the bank, the operation was looking feasible. We both thought Suzy would share our relief. Instead she chose that moment to announce that she was driving down to Kent for a long weekend. We tried to talk her out of it, of course, but she got her way, as she always did.

She was an obstinate little bitch. Sharp, too. She'd obviously considered the possibility that I could take the money and run. It was strange to find myself using the same argument to reassure her as Mike had used on me earlier. It made me wonder whether he meant it any more than I did. And then her splendid notion that I should double-cross Mike and take all the money! The irony of that appealed to me. Here she was, urging me to think about dumping Mike, when I was thinking how easy it was going to be to dump her!

I wasn't actually angry about Suzy's departure; that would have taken more energy than I had. If nothing else she'd made me realize how much I needed a break myself. Mike took the interruption less gracefully. After two weeks of relentless activity he couldn't cope with the ensuing vacuum. He mooched around the flat, tidying this and straightening that. Then he perched on the sofa and picked up a newspaper. I thought he was going to settle down to read it but two minutes later he was on his feet again. This time he came back with a carpet sweeper and I had to get up so that he could brush the carpet—more vigorously, it seemed to me, than was necessary. When he'd finished that he put all the furniture back to where it was two weeks ago, before we cleared the centre of the lounge for practice runs. I didn't say anything but we were only going to have to move it again when we resumed on Tuesday. That must have dawned on him too because he had second thoughts and rearranged all the furniture once more. I dropped into an armchair while he was putting things away and he came back and stood in the centre of the room, looking round and chewing the inside of his cheek. I waited. Finally he said he couldn't see much point in hanging around: Suzy had gone to see her parents; he might just as well go down to Dagenham and spend the weekend with his. I nodded. He put a few things together and I heard the front door open and close behind him.

Suddenly it all seemed very peaceful. The only sound I could hear was the faint swish of traffic on the street outside.

I stayed in the flat. I think I must have slept most of the time. I don't know why I was so exhausted. We'd done an awful lot of projections in the last couple of weeks, though, and I was beginning to wonder if it was having a cumulative effect on me. Going into resonance hadn't seemed to do the rat any harm, but we'd only tested it with a few projections. I'd done dozens by now.

*

There must be an art to coaching. Olympic athletes have to be at their best in time for the Games. A football team has to work like a well-oiled machine when they go into a major Cup match. Well, whatever that talent was, Mike didn't have it. His solution was just to drive us harder. We were back together on Tuesday evening, rehearsing intensively, to no good purpose. Our times were getting worse, not better. We'd missed our peak. In spite of the break we were stale.

Wednesday came, and after practising for the whole evening we sat round the kitchen table, bleary-eyed, saying nothing, just picking at yet another take-away. Mike pushed himself away from the table.

"All right. It's crunch time. Do we go in tomorrow or not?"

He looked from me to Suzy and back again. Of the three of us, he still seemed to have the most energy.

I toyed with an expanded polystyrene tray full of luke-warm noodles.

"We've prepared pretty well," I said. "I don't think we'll ever be more ready than we are now."

"Suzy?"

"Well if we don't go tomorrow it's another two weeks before the next delivery. I don't think I could take another two weeks of this."

"Okay. Tomorrow it is. Rodge, we're going to have to go in at six-thirty to get the equipment warmed up. Is that going to be a problem?"

"Christ, Mike, can't we..? Look, I don't think so. I'll just use my card key. There's no one at the security desk at that time and even if we run into a patrol it won't be the first time they've seen me coming and going at odd hours. If they ask, well, we've simply got a long experiment to do, and we're starting early because we want to get away tonight for the Bank Holiday."

"If that happens it won't look good if we walk out at lunch-time."

"No, all right, we'll have to go back to the flat later in the day. But I don't think it's going to happen. Okay?"

Suzy clapped her hands over her ears.

"Oh, I'm so sick of it! 'If this, if that.' I just wish the whole thing were over and done with!"

Mike's mouth set.

"It will be soon enough, Suzy, and then you can relax. You'll be a wealthy young lady."

41

However hard you try to cover every eventuality, it seems there's always something you overlook. Mike and I were poised and ready to go, waiting for Suzy's phone call, and it was already several minutes past eight. Our precious margin was beginning to evaporate. I was waiting tensely in the cage, holding the duffel bag. I was wearing the balaclava, the gun was in its holster, the pillow case was in my pocket, and precut lengths of rope were looped through my belt. Mike was waiting by the control panel, biting his lip. We both jumped when his mobile sounded.

He listened for a moment. Then:

"For Chrissake! All right, get back as fast as you can. Rodge will meet you there."

He clicked off the phone. His voice was taut.

"She had to call us from the ladies' loo. Couldn't get any reception in the secure area—must be some sort of steel reinforcement in the walls. Let's get moving."

I heard the relay engage and immediately I was aware of a juxtaposition of unfamiliar surroundings. There was something dark in front of me. I concentrated hard on it and the outline of the cage faded away. I was in the secure area and I was looking at the open safe. Suzy was supposed to be here, getting things ready, but of course there was no one around. I stepped forward and looked inside the safe. It was almost full of heavy-duty polythene bags. I reached in and grabbed the nearest one, tore open the seal and started transferring the money to my open duffel bag. I couldn't hold the duffel bag open properly so I had to pull out the bundles of notes and stuff them in. I knew we were losing time but I didn't dare stop to check my watch. The door buzzer went. The gun was in my hand in an instant. The door opened and I relaxed. It was Suzy.

"Sorry, sorry..." she said under her breath, leaving the door to close behind her and hurrying over. I said nothing.

It was a lot easier with Suzy pulling the money bags out and up-ending them into the duffel, just as we'd practised in the flat. She emptied the last of this batch and tossed in the mobile phone, as we'd instructed her. I closed the flap and signalled Mike to return me to the cage. It felt like we'd overrun badly on the first trip and with the late start that wasn't a good omen. Mike was ready by the door of the cage with the empty duffel bag and I exchanged it for the full one. He'd already flipped the switches to recharge the capacitor bank. He ran quickly round to the control panel, and I could just make out his movements as he adjusted the voltage, brought the power up with the sliders, and pressed the red button. The relay clonked and I was back in the secure area ready to fill the duffel bag for the second time.

We completed the second trip, then the third, fourth and fifth. It was going more smoothly now. We'd fallen into a rhythm, just like when we were rehearsing in the first week. I stole a quick look at my watch as I was preparing to return from trip number six; it was seventeen minutes past eight, almost back on schedule. Then the door buzzer sounded.

Suzy froze. I ducked behind her, the gun already in my hand. Nadine didn't see me immediately.

"Oh, Suzy. Caroline asked me to tell you..."

She was far enough into the room for me to jump out and gesture to her with the gun. She didn't move; she'd gone rigid with shock. It was a self-closing door but I moved between it and Nadine just the same and shoved her roughly towards Suzy. That way I could keep both of them covered with the gun, as if Suzy, too, was an innocent party. Nadine was watching me with wide dark eyes, those big front teeth on her lower lip. She started to make little whimpering noises. I turned her around and gave her a sharp poke with the gun to move her on; I thought it would be best to put her where we could keep an eye on her. Then I hissed at her in my rough South London accent:

"No' a sound! On the floor, feet togevver, hands behind yer back. DO IT!"

I used the precut lengths of rope to tie her wrists and ankles, as we'd rehearsed many times, only I probably pulled them a lot tighter because I was really irritated by the interruption. Then I put the pillow case over her head and kept it in place with another length of rope around her neck. At least I remembered to leave that one loose. I was still on one knee. Without pausing or even moving I signalled Mike. An instant later I was back in the cage, handing over the sixth bag. We had about five minutes left and I still had two bags to fill and Suzy to tie up.

What with the effort and the tension and the damned balaclava I was getting overheated. I tried to wipe the sweat out of my eyes with my sleeve as I went in for the seventh time. We'd done a really quick turn-round in the lab but Suzy was slowing up; she didn't yet have all the bags out of the safe and open. She was obviously getting tired. I didn't dare to say anything in case Nadine overheard so I just gritted my teeth and worked at the slower pace. Suzy straightened up wearily and Mike transported me back to the cage with the full duffel. Just one more trip to go.

The relay went clonk for the eighth time and I was back in the secure area. I held the duffel bag open and Suzy shook in one lot of money. As she was doing it I turned my wrist to glance at my watch. It was already eight-twenty six. This was no good; there wouldn't be enough time to tie Suzy up. There was a quicker way.

I socked her as she straightened up to get another bag. She staggered back, hand half-raised to her jaw, eyes wide with surprise. I was punching only half my weight and I realized straight away that I hadn't hit her hard enough, so as she bounced off the safe and came forward I clocked her again, coming up from a crouch and turning my body to get plenty of weight on it. The blow caught her on the jaw, almost lifting her, and the force of it carried her right round towards the door. She back-pedalled, hit the door, and collapsed there in a tangle of limbs. I didn't give her a second glance but quickly grabbed the next polythene bag, tipping it over the duffel without caring what spilt around it, threw the empty money bag down and reached for another, tipped that too, and then I froze, the empty bag still in my hands. The alarm had gone off. It was a terrible noise, a rising and falling raucous screaming that filled my head. *How the hell did they...?*

I decided to get out of there. The sound level was tremendous; I couldn't think straight. I tried to focus my awareness on the cage and succeeded in bringing up the angular outline of the frame but in my muddled vision it was still floating over the entrance door to the secure area, with Suzy's inert form lying in front of it. I was so confused I probably raised my arm in both places. Nothing happened;

the two visuals were still shifting and overlapping. Then my view of the cage sharpened for a brief moment and I saw Mike. But Mike wasn't at the control panel, and he wasn't at the door. He was standing just outside the cage, putting a mobile phone back into his pocket. I thought I saw his lips move, but I couldn't hear a thing for the racket. And then my awareness shifted into the secure area again but only the bottom half of the door was visible now and I saw that the shutter was coming down and I felt myself sucked towards it in a blinding explosion of heat and light…

42

Well you didn't think I'd let him get away with it, did you? Rodge, my so-called best friend. The bastard. I was waiting for her, waiting so patiently. She said she'd had a bad relationship, so I made allowances, wanting her, aching for her, but holding back until she was ready. And then in walks Rodge and she goes to him like a moth to a flame. To make it worse the pair of them carry on in my own flat. It's not that big a flat. At night I could hear the rhythmic thumping, and her crying out in pleasure or pain as he went at her. Two or three times a night. And I pulled the pillow over my head and cried with the hurt and the grief and the frustration of it, and swore my time would come.

I didn't have to rush it; I could afford to wait for the perfect opportunity. The bit of business to get Meredrew was a good confidence-builder. Rodge was obsessed with that, so he didn't need any persuading, and it had the added advantage of getting Suzy to dip her toe in some muddy water. After that it wasn't hard to get them both interested in the bigger plan, especially with the amount of money involved. That's when I saw my chance. I told them it was the perfect crime. They thought I meant the perfect robbery. I meant the perfect murder.

The shutter was made of molybdenum-coated steel. It wasn't difficult to establish that after I'd asked Suzy to make a note of the manufacturer's label. I simply rang them up, posing as a jeweller who wanted to make his stock more secure.

"Oh, yes, sir, all of our shutters have the same construction; the only difference is the size. We'd be happy to come and measure up for you. Yes, molybdenum coating on all steel parts, we standardized on that some time ago. It's why they're so durable. You can buy shutters of cheaper manufacture, of course, but you'll have to replace them after a few years, and then it's not cheaper any more, is it? If you buy one of ours it's guaranteed for twenty years. It won't wear and it'll keep its appearance permanently."

Well, it will unless you belt a matter wave beam through it.

It's funny how Rodge was worried what I might do when I had seven bags in front of me. I thought it was a nice touch to let it get exactly that far. Then I projected him back for the last bag. I waited for a few moments and then I punched the number into my mobile and said, in a calm but urgent voice:

"Police here. We've been told there's a robbery in progress at your branch. Would you please activate the alarm immediately? We'll have a car there in a few minutes."

I even heard the Bank's alarm siren starting up before I clicked off. The part of Rodge that was still in the cage hadn't caught what I was saying, of course; all his attention was focused at the other end. Not that it would have mattered if he had heard something; he couldn't have done anything about it. He started to lift his arm up and down frantically as I was putting the mobile back in my pocket. I said, "Goodbye, Rodge." I caught a glimpse of the panic in his eyes and then he'd gone.

Only not completely. On the seat where he'd been a moment ago was a brain. His brain. It looked like a wrinkled blancmange, sagging a little under its own weight, still quivering from having landed there. Coiled behind it was a glistening white rope and the whole chair was enmeshed in a mass of cobwebby strands. And then I remembered what had happened to the spider when I'd dropped the molybdenum steel sample into the matter wave beam, and the greyish-white blobs it left behind. Spiders don't have a brain as such but they do have a nervous system, so the blobs must have been the larger ganglia. Wasn't that interesting? There was something different about the matter waves involved in transporting nervous tissue; for some reason they didn't get absorbed. So when the rest of his body went, the muscles and bones and blood and organs and everything were absorbed but his nervous system got left behind. It was there now, draped all over his chair.

The more I thought about it the more it made sense. That's how he could transfer his awareness back and forth between the other place and the cage: his brain never left the cage! For a moment I stood there, staring at it. Such a clever brain. But not quite clever enough.

I'd taken the precaution of turning off the cooling water supply in the main electricity cables, and things were cooking nicely by now. The shutter in the bank vault had put a colossal drain on power when it absorbed the matter waves, so circuits had melted and everything was starting to overload. I stood there, calmly watching as the needles went off-scale on all the dials, and smoke started to pour out of the housings. There was a ripping sound of arcing electricity and one of the power supplies exploded, shooting out a rain of fiery fragments. Then another one went, and another. Some cables caught fire and it quickly spread into the cage. I strolled round and opened the cage door to give it a decent draught. Things were still exploding and chunks of burning plastic were flying out in every direction, trailing smoke behind them. I backed slowly towards the door.

A tongue of flame uncurled across the floor, following some unseen track. On the other side of the lab it licked up a wooden bench, outlining in sudden relief two retort stands, with a length of rope clamped between them, and two weights, suspended on strings—the pendulums Rodge had used when he first explained coupled mass resonance to me. Then the strings burned through, the weights fell in a shower of sparks, and the flames fanned out over the bench. And at that point I left.

I waited in the gents toilet upstairs. There weren't any smoke detectors or sprinklers in the basement so the fire was well established before anyone sounded the alarm. When they evacuated the building I just went out with the crowd. The fire engines were rolling up as I walked away, the money safely stowed in my sports bag. I guessed the crews would have a bit of a job on their hands but they'd probably get it under control. By the time they did there wouldn't be much left of the lab. Of course that would just be the beginning. There'd be a whole slew of inquiries and, as Dean, poor old Professor Ledsham would bear the brunt of it. I could imagine the conversations he'd be having with the police.

"You know, Professor, the blaze was very nearly out of control. You were very lucky the Fire Service was able to deal with it before it spread to the rest of the building. It seems there weren't any sprinklers installed down there."

"No, well there wouldn't be, Superintendent. It was an electrical lab."

"The laboratory was in use, then?"

"Only temporarily, some time ago. The basement area

was due for refurbishment in the next phase of the Estates Plan. In the meantime I had a Ph.D. student working in there. It was the only place that had an adequate power supply for what he was doing. After he qualified he stayed on for a short while."

"You're talking about Rodger Dukas?"

"Yes, how did you know?"

"We checked with the School Administration Office, sir. He was still on the records. You said he stayed on for a short while. Did he tell you when he was leaving?"

"No. That would have been a conventional courtesy, of course, but Dukas wasn't a conventional student. And I haven't been down there for a while, myself. Far too much to do up here. I'm afraid I don't know when he left."

"Well, Professor, this may come as a shock to you, but we don't think he'd left at all. In fact we think he was in there when the fire started."

"What? My God! Did he get out?"

"Probably not. The fire inspection team said there was a lot of burning plastic and other material. He could have been overcome by toxic fumes."

"Oh, this is unbelievable! I mean, he was an unusual student—a bit lacking in social skills, to be honest—but there's no denying he was extremely capable. It would be a— look, how sure are you about this? Did you find a, er, any evidence that, er…"

"No, sir. The fire was so intense it left nothing behind. But we've checked the security cameras on the front entrance. A man answering the description of the Rodger Dukas in your records was seen entering at six-thirty in the morning on the day of the accident, carrying a sports bag and what looks like a squash racket. Someone came in with him, also

259

carrying a bag and a racket. We assume it was his squash partner but as yet we don't know who it was. Probably they arranged to meet later in the day. We found the remains of a squash racquet in the lab, which suggests that Dukas had been there."

"But surely he could have left before the fire started?"

"We think not. As you know, sir, he's tall, fair-haired, very distinctive. Our people have been through the footage from those security cameras with a fine-toothed comb and he didn't show up again."

"But he could have been elsewhere in the building at the time, couldn't he? Then he would have got out with all the others when the fire alarm went off."

"We thought of that. We showed his picture to everyone who was in the building that day and nobody remembers seeing him. In any case, all the evidence points to a major equipment overload as the cause of the fire, which means there must have been some sort of experiment in progress down there. If he wasn't running it, who was? And the fact remains, he hasn't been seen since."

"Have you tried his flat?"

"Yes. We sent an officer to the address on your records but nobody was there. In fact it had been cleared out. The landlord wasn't very pleased. He said the rent hadn't been paid for some time."

"He might have gone home. It was a bank holiday weekend."

"We checked with the next of kin. He wasn't there and they weren't expecting him. Tell me, Professor, do you know what Dukas was doing in that lab?"

And of course, poor old Professor Ledsham would go on to explain that Rodge was continuing his investigations into the effect of electromagnetic radiation on living organisms.

No one would ever know what really went on.

I kept the GPS receiver, but I wiped the memory. It wouldn't have been a good idea to keep the GPS coordinates of about thirty unsolved crimes in there. Back in the flat I found the notebooks with all Rodge's calculations. I'm not clever enough to understand them, but it seemed sensible to remove them before I disposed of the rest of his stuff. He hadn't told anyone he was coming in with me, and I sure as hell hadn't told my landlord, so they wouldn't have a clue where he'd been living.

I think I've had my fill of research. I mean, after what I was doing with Rodge anything else would be an anticlimax. Maybe one day people will do it again, and travel to the other side of the globe in an instant, or to the moon or the planets. We were just ahead of our time, that's all, Rodge and me. I really ought to write it all down, just to prove we were the first to do it. Maybe I could write a book about it, except of course there's no way I could ever publish it.

I rang Suzy's own mobile after a while but there was no answer. Later on I tried to get her at her flat, but she wasn't there, and Siobhan hadn't seen her. There was something on the news the following morning. They hadn't released her name yet but it was pretty obvious what had happened. The Fire Brigade had gone in to remove what was left of the shutter and when they did they found her body. I don't know whether it was the enormous heat from the melting shutter that killed her, or a lungful of smoke and molybdenum vapour. I hadn't meant for her to get hurt. I was kind of hoping that with Rodge out of the way we could pick up where we left off, leave the country, perhaps go to Costa Rica or something. After all, I had getting on for two million in cash. Still, I suppose she brought it on herself, and if I'm honest I never really felt the same way about her after Rodge started humping her.

I don't know who the other girl was. The TV crew filmed her Mum and Dad and two sisters outside the hospital; they'd come down from Oldham to see her. I suppose when Rodge tied her up he left her further away from the shutter, so she survived, although she had to be treated for smoke inhalation and burns on her legs from flying gobs of molten metal. It was just as well her head was inside a pillow case at the time. It sounds like she wasn't badly hurt. Anyway she's lucky to have such a nice supportive family.

If they ever track me down, I'll just say I was an old friend, and yes, I did pay him a visit in his lab and played squash with him once or twice, but no, I didn't understand what he was doing, all that stuff was well beyond me, sorry.

But I'm not going to wait around for that to happen. Apart from anything else, I can't spend the money here without attracting attention. No, I'll go abroad like we planned to do in the first place. I fancy Australia but I hear they have some mammoth spiders there so I might try for New Zealand instead. They should accept me. After all, it's not as if I'm unqualified; I do have a B.Sc. in Physics—oh, and by the way, I passed my exams, so I now have an M.Sc. in Inventions and the Law as well, for what that's worth. Not to mention more than adequate finance.

I'll attend Rodge's memorial service before I leave, though. I like to do the right thing.

EPILOGUE

So here I am, still in the queue, with one person left in front of me. Now that it's all over and people have paid their respects, most of them have gone home. A few have stayed on, though, standing around quietly or talking in low voices. One or two are looking up at the grey sky from time to time to see if it's going to rain and I'm still trying to think of what I'm going to say. And now the person in front of me is moving away and suddenly here I am, standing in front of her.

Rodger's Mum.

Mrs. Dukas.

She has a sort of empathic smile, like she already knows what I'll be trying to say. And she extends her hand to me, and it seems awfully small, like a little bird, so I have to be careful not to squeeze it, because I can be a bit clumsy like that.

"Er, hallo, Mrs. Dukas. I'm Michael. I was a friend. I'm very sorry."

ALSO AVAILABLE FROM FINGERPRESS:

Raoul, fat Head Chef of Le Metro, the top hotel of Paris, hardly notices the Nazi invaders occupying the city – until they threaten his beloved demi-sous chef Natalie.

From acclaimed author Fredrik Nath, *The Fat Chef* is a wartime tale of unrequited love, heroism, and a rather suspect Béchamel sauce.

www.fingerpress.co.uk/the-fat-chef

*A captivating novel – and its sequel – from
Hugo-nominated author Dominic Green*

Mount Ararat, a world the size of an asteroid yet with Earth-standard gravity, plays host to an eccentric farming community protected by the Devil, a mechanical killing machine, from such passers-by as Mr von Trapp (an escapee from a penal colony), the Made (manufactured humans being hunted by the State), and the super-rich clients of a gravitational health spa established at Mount Ararat's South Pole.

www.fingerpress.co.uk/smallworld
www.fingerpress.co.uk/littlestar

CPSIA information can be obtained at www.ICGtesting.com
Printed in the USA
BVOW05s2004040914

365557BV00002B/9/P

9 781908 824400